Gunner

Nicola Jane

Copyright © 2019 by Nicola Jane

Copyright © 2023 by Nicola Jane

All rights reserved.

No portion of this book may be reproduced in any form without written permission from the publisher or author, except as permitted by U.K. copyright law.

Meet The Team

Cover design: Francessca Wingfield @ Wingfield Designs
Editor: Rebecca Vazquez, Dark Syde Books
Formatting: Nicola Miller

Disclaimer:
This book is a work of fiction. The names, characters, places, and incidents are all products of the author's imagination and are not to be construed as real. Any similarities are entirely coincidental.

Spelling:
Please note, this author resides in the United Kingdom and is using British English. Therefore, some words may be viewed as incorrect or spelled incorrectly. However, they are not.

Trigger Warning

This book contains triggers, including cheating. If you are sensitive to triggers, avoid this book.

Contents

Playlist	VII
PROLOGUE	1
CHAPTER ONE	4
CHAPTER TWO	20
CHAPTER THREE	32
CHAPTER FOUR	42
CHAPTER FIVE	54
CHAPTER SIX	68
CHAPTER SEVEN	77
CHAPTER EIGHT	91
CHAPTER NINE	100
CHAPTER TEN	115
CHAPTER ELEVEN	128
CHAPTER TWELVE	140
CHAPTER THIRTEEN	156
CHAPTER FOURTEEN	173
EPILOGUE	178

1. Read a sample of Cooper by Nicola Jane   181

A note from me to you   191

Popular Books By Nicola Jane   192

Playlist

Glimpse of Us – Joji

omw – trash.man

Prove Me Right – Alex Amor

X&Y – Caity Baser

One Foot in Front of the Other – Griff

Remember (Acoustic) – Becky Hill

that way – Tate McRae

Shouldn't Be thinking About You – Jamie Grey

Boyfriend Of The Year – Bellah Mae

How Could You – Jessie Murph

Back to Friends – Lauren Spencer-Smith

Better Days (Acoustic) – Dermot Kennedy

Come Back Home – Sofia Carson

I Didn't Know – Sofia Carson

PROLOGUE

Ava

I smile as I read the text, then hold the phone to my chest. "What are you so happy about?" asks Damien suspiciously. I glance at my seventeen-year-old brother and then shove my phone into my back pocket. He isn't above snatching it to read my texts.

"I've been invited to Charlotte's party tonight."

"No," he says firmly.

I roll my eyes and turn my attention to my dad, who's got his head in paperwork. "Pops, please, can I go?" He looks at my brother, and Damien shakes his head.

"No," Dad says, returning his attention back to the paperwork.

"It's your decision, not Damien's," I screech, the injustice at being denied a social event at thirteen years of age clearly clouding my judgement to win my dad over.

Dad gives me an annoyed look. "Isn't Charlotte the girl who always throws ridiculous parties whenever her parents go out of town?"

"Pops, she's fourteen and giving head better than the club girls," says Gunner, my brother's best friend, rolling his eyes.

I glower at him. "Why are you even getting involved, Gunner? Pops, please."

He shakes his head, finality in his eyes, and I stamp my foot, storming off to my bedroom. I take out my phone and look at the text again. The address is only a half-hour bus ride, so I type a quick reply saying I'll be there at six. I can sneak out, and Dad and Damien will assume that I've gone to bed early in a huff, and I can be back in bed by midnight. They'll never even know.

At exactly six that evening, I stand in front of the paint-chipped door and glance around nervously. I pull out my phone again and check I have the right address. I was expecting the guy I've been speaking to for weeks to have a nice house. The way he spoke made me think he came from money. Not that it makes a difference, of course. I agreed to meet him because I liked him, not because of money, but still, this place creeps me out and looks a little abandoned. Before I can talk myself out of it, I raise my fist and knock on the door.

When there's no answer, I knock again, this time louder. There's no one about. The street is empty, and across the way is an old factory building that has been abandoned for years. I take a deep breath and make my way around the side of the property.

I send off a text, letting him know I'm here and asking where he is. A few seconds later, I get a text back, and I frown in confusion when I read the words, ***Behind you, baby***.

As I turn to look, a body slams against mine. I'm swept off my feet and held around the waist. I open my mouth to scream right as a cloth is pressed against my face, and I have no choice but to inhale the strong fumes coating the rag. It all happens so fast that my brain is struggling to process what's happening, and as it hits me that I've been tricked, I feel my body go heavy and my eyes close.

CHAPTER ONE

10 Years later...
Ava

I let out a deep sigh. My best friend, Chloe, is hanging off the arm of a random guy who's trying to make his way home. He looks irritated by her drunken slurring, but I have to give him credit, he's being extremely patient with her.

"I mean, I'm really not that bad, am I?" she cries, stumbling for the third time since holding on to him. "Besides, who else would put up with that? He cheated so many times."

I take pity on the guy and grab Chloe's hand, halting her so that her arm drops from his. I give him a grateful smile. "Thanks for being her walking aide. I'm really sorry again." He smiles politely and shrugs before carrying on his journey. "Seriously, Chlo, you have to stop this. You won't ever find another man if all you go on about is Darren. The self-pity is a definite turnoff. Even I'm turned off."

Chloe broke up with Darren after a year together. The relationship was unhealthy, to say the least. There were constant arguments and tears over Darren's infidelity, and I'm almost certain he cheated way more than the three times she'd discovered. Needless to say, he met someone else and ended things with her. She's still devastated two months on. Tonight was about spending time with the girls, so Chloe could forget about Darren, but she's spent the entire night crying and talking about him and all the terrible things he did or said. I felt sorry for the other girls, who were getting tired of hearing about it. There's only so much consoling you can do before you just want to have fun, so I sent them clubbing and offered to get Chloe home.

"It's alright for you, surrounded by those gorgeous bikers all day. Some of us aren't privileged enough to have hot gang members to save us."

I roll eyes. "You know damn well the guys are more like brothers to me, and you also know how annoying it is to be surrounded by so many suffocating, overprotective big brothers. Besides, you've had your fair share of flirtatious moments with the guys, especially Damien."

Damien, my actual blood big brother, is President of The Eagles Motorcycle Club. He's the typical biker lover's wet dream. He's tall and well-built, and tattoos cover his arms, the artwork all club-related. His dark hair is shaved around the sides and he sports a small man bun. The darkness of his hair and his deep tan make his dark blue eyes so piercing, everyone comments on them when they first meet him. He's never had a problem with the ladies, much to Chloe's annoyance, because she's lusted after him since she was a teenager.

My father is a founding member of the club. When he came out of the Army thirty years ago, he found life without his military brothers difficult. So, he started the club with two Army buddies, both of whom have now passed—one to an illness and the other to drink—leaving my father as the only living founding member. The rest of the guys respect him, and everyone refers to him as 'Pops' because he's like a father to everyone in the club.

"Damien doesn't give two shits about me," slurs Chloe, and I roll my eyes. She's so dramatic when she's drunk.

"You got together with Darren, so Damien backed off. You're drunk and trying to pick an argument. Let's get you home to sober up."

Chloe fumbles about in her pocket, pulling out her mobile phone. "I'm going to ring him."

"Damien?" I ask, confused as to why she would ring him at this hour, especially since he doesn't know I'm out on the town.

"No, silly. Darren. I need to hear his voice."

I groan. If she continues like this, the guy will end up getting a restraining order against her. I take the phone from her hand and shove it in my pocket. Chloe yells in protest as I drag her towards a cab. I wave frantically, but the driver pulls away from the side of the road. He clearly thinks Chloe is too drunk, and he's right, of course.

A car slows to a stop alongside us and the window lowers slowly. I bend down to look inside and stare into the furious eyes of Maddocks, the Eagles Enforcer. I wince because Damien thinks I'm working a shift at Emzie's as a favour to Emma, my other best friend.

"Ava, what the hell are you doing staggering around at this time of morning? Does D know you're out?" I stay silent, and he groans. "Jesus Christ, he doesn't know?"

I shake my head and press my lips together in what I hope looks cute and cheeky. "He might think I'm at Emzie's tonight."

It's not that Damien's against me going out and having a social life, but he likes to know about it, and he always sends at least one of the guys to tag along at a distance to keep a watchful eye on me.

"Get the fuck in the car. Look at the state of her," he growls, referring to Chloe, who's wobbling all over the place. We slide into the back and Chloe immediately lays down, placing her head on my lap. I stroke her long blonde hair, and her light snores fill the car before we've even pulled back into traffic.

"I have to go to the train station first. Got a pick-up to do," says Maddocks, his cold brown eyes catching mine in the rear-view mirror.

"Okay, anyone I know?"

"Yep, I'd say so." I can see the smile in his eyes. "A certain green-eyed solider."

I inhale sharply, my heart rate suddenly picking up and the blood whooshing in my ears. Gunner is coming home. *Why didn't anyone tell me? Why didn't Damien say something?*

"You okay there, baby girl?" There's concern on his face, but I just nod, not trusting myself to speak.

Gunner . . . Ashton Gunn is Vice President of the club. He's spent the last couple years in Afghanistan with the Army. This will be the second time I've seen him since I had my daughter, Evelyn, who's now two years old. The first time he came back, she was just about to turn one, and he wasn't overly impressed to discover I'd become a mother. I had begged Damien not to tell him while he was away as I didn't think it was fair to distract him when he was on tour. If anything had happened to him, I would never have forgiven myself.

We'd all grown up together in the club, though I was the annoying little sister, being four years younger. Damien and Gunner were closer than any of the brothers, and everyone joked that they were mini versions of our dads, so it was no surprise they stepped into their shoes with no fuss. And although no one knew, I was madly in love with Gunner.

But as we got older, things changed. I went off to university to study nursing and I lived on campus, much to Damien's annoyance. I wanted to get away from the stifling club, and watching Gunner with other women was ripping me apart. I'd return every few months for holidays and did my best to stay out of Gunner's way. And then he joined the armed forces, so once I graduated, I moved back home.

My thoughts are interrupted when the car comes to a stop, and I notice we're outside the train station. A large Hulk-like figure steps out of the shadows. At around six-foot, he's intimidating by size alone, and my stomach does a somersault. He still has the ability to do that to me without knowing it. As he steps into the light of the streetlamp, with a bag flung over his shoulder, I beg my heart to stop wanting him, because despite distance and time apart, I still feel exactly the same as I did all those years ago.

I take in his strong, muscled arms straining through his tight black T-shirt. His chiselled jaw is covered in a nine o'clock shadow, making his piercing green eyes stand out against his sun-kissed skin.

His gaze fixes on me and his step falters. I look away, embarrassed he caught me gawking like a lovesick teenager.

The front passenger door opens and he bends down to look in. "Brother, long time no see." He grins, shaking hands with Maddocks.

"Fuck me, Gunner, the size of you seems to have tripled," Maddocks greets him.

He gets in to the car and turns in his seat, glancing over me and Chloe. "This my homecoming present?" He grins, turning back around to face the front.

The fact that he only acknowledges me as a piece of arse makes my heart ache. "No, man, you remember Ava and don't pretend you don't," says Maddocks as he manoeuvres the vehicle back out into the traffic.

"'Course, yeah, sorry, Ava."

He knew it was me. He's playing the game again, the one where he acts like I don't exist. You'd think a year would be long enough to get over it, but I know deep down, the real reason is because, three years ago, we shared a night together. Since then, he's treated me differently, like he hates my guts.

"She thought she'd be clever and sneak out tonight. I found the pair of them staggering by the road, thumbing for a lift. Pres is gonna kill her," Maddocks tells him.

"Thought she had a kid now? Tell me she ain't one of them mums who puts partying over her kid," Gunner replies.

"I'm a damn good mother and don't ever question that," I snap, and the men exchange a look. "And for the record, I'm an adult. I can leave the club anytime I want."

"Still a spitfire with a mouth loud enough to wake the dead," Gunner mutters, smirking at Maddocks. I roll my eyes, refusing to get into this with him. He needs to get over himself.

"It's good to have you back, man. D was so happy when you called tonight. Why'd you leave it so late to tell us?" asks Maddocks.

I see his huge shoulders shrug. "Last minute thing."

"Are you back for long?"

"Undecided."

I frown. Usually, leave is agreed by the Army, and you know when you're coming home and when you're going back. His short answers tell me he doesn't want to talk about it.

We pull into the car park of the clubhouse. It's situated on an old industrial estate next to the railway line. Part of a large complex, the club owns all the land and the buildings on it. I wake Chloe, and she sits up sleepily. "Where are we?"

"The clubhouse."

We get out and she realises there's another body with us before shrieking and running at Gunner, throwing herself into his waiting arms. He swings her around and a stab of jealousy pricks my heart. I remember a time when he used to treat me like that. Now, he can barely look at me.

"How's things, gorgeous?" he asks, kissing her cheek.

Chloe glows under his compliment, hooking arms with him and leading him inside with me tailing behind. All the guys think Chloe is gorgeous, and she is, with her long blonde hair and a backside and boobs that most girls would pay for. She's the perfect combination of sweet and fun.

Inside, the place is full. Everyone must have heard about Gunner's return . . . everyone but me. Gemma, Rooster's ol' lady, rushes over to me, ignoring the crowd now surrounding Gunner.

"I tried to call you to warn you," she whisper-hisses. She's one of the few ol' ladies around my age.

I give a fake smile. "It's fine. Chloe was a mess, so I didn't get a chance to check my phone. Where's Damien?"

My question is soon answered when the office door at the back of the club swings open and Damien fills it with his bulky frame.

"Some fucker told me you were back," he thunders, his voice causing everyone else to quiet down. He heads towards Gunner and slaps him on the back before pulling him into a hug. "Good to have you back, big guy."

As I'm heading for the bar with Gemma, Damien clocks me. "Where the fuck have you been? And don't try that bullshit about Emzie's because I went in there and you weren't working."

"I went out with Chloe instead. Don't make a deal out of it." Gunner's watching me closely and it's making me uncomfortable.

"All I ask is you tell me, so I can get someone on you. It's for your safety."

I roll my eyes. "The last thing I need on a night out is one of your cockblocks in a leather jacket. I went all through Uni and lived to tell the tale."

"But got pregnant by a guy who didn't stick around," chimes in Gunner, arching a brow.

"And suddenly you remember me," I say, my words dripping in sarcasm. "Enjoy the welcome home brigade," I add, referring to the club girls circling him like he's their next prey.

Gemma joins me along with Chloe. "Evie was a superstar tonight. She went straight to bed with no fuss."

I smile at her gratefully. "Thanks for having her. I really appreciate it."

Tap hands us a bottle of gin. I also take a pint of water for Chloe, and we move ourselves to a table in the corner.

Occasionally, I sneak glances over at Gunner. It's like he's never been away, he's laughing and drinking with the guys like it's a normal Saturday night. This is the longest I've been around him since I spent that one night in his bed, and it's harder than when he's away, not knowing where or how he is.

I often think about our night together, and I wondered for months if he did too. But looking at the way he is now, flirting with the club girls, I can see it was something I'd told myself to try and console my broken heart. The morning after that night was the morning Gunner crushed my heart into a billion pieces by telling me it was a huge mistake and he'd only wanted one last night of fun before going off to the Army. I thought I'd finally gotten my dream, but all it really was, was a one-night stand.

I finish my drink and ask, "Chlo, do you want me to help you to bed?" She stays so often at the clubhouse that she has her own room.

"No, you go to bed. You have work tomorrow. I'm going to have another drink with Gem."

I quietly push open my bedroom door. Evie is spread out like a starfish on my bed, her brown hair fanned out around her like a crown. I smile to myself. As hard as it is being a single parent, I love this girl with all my heart. I have it easier than most because I have all the club, and every one of them love this little girl like their own.

I'm standing in the doorway, lost in thought, when heavy footsteps catch my attention. Gunner stops at the top of the stairs, staring at me like a deer caught in headlights. He continues towards his room, but as he passes me, he slows, catching a glimpse of Evelyn.

"She got big."

I nod, folding my arms. "She's growing fast."

"Have you been okay?" he asks, walking backwards to keep eye contact until he reaches his door.

I nod. "Yeah, have you?" When he's like this—normal, without anyone around—my heart begs me to tell him how I really feel.

He shrugs a shoulder and puts the key in his lock, clicking it until the door opens. "Good to see yah, Bait." And then he's gone, closing his door quietly. *Bait.* He's called my that since I turned eighteen, though I never got to the bottom of why.

I'm awoken suddenly and I sit up quickly, looking around, wondering what woke me. Then I hear a low moan followed by a shout. I glance down, and Evie is still flat out next to me, her little body sprawled out peacefully. The moaning continues. I groan, needing to find the source of the noise and mute it before it wakes Evie.

I pull on my silk robe and step out into the hall. It doesn't take me long to realise the noise is coming from Gunner's room. I listen for a minute, praying he hasn't got a woman in there. A painful cry rings out into the silence and the nurse in me takes over. Before I know it,

I'm standing in his room, staring down at him as he thrashes around on his bed, his sheets tangled around him.

Approaching the bed cautiously, I know I can't wake him suddenly as it could cause more damage to him and to me. "Gunner," I whisper, "it's Ava. Wake up." He doesn't respond and doesn't slow his thrashing arms. "Ashton," I say, a little firmer this time, and he stills. "Wake up." He bolts upright, scaring the life out of me, and I yelp in surprise, jumping back.

"Cammie?" he gasps.

I ignore the hurt at hearing him call for another woman. It's not like he's been celibate the last few years. In fact, it reminds me I know nothing about him now. "No, it's Ava. Sorry," I whisper. "You were having a bad dream. I just thought I'd check on you."

"I'm fine," he snaps, making me flinch. He scrubs his hands over his face and releases a long breath. Then he throws his legs over the edge of the bed, unwrapping them from the sheets and throwing them behind him angrily. "Fuck," he mutters to himself.

"Sorry, it sounded like you were in pain. I'll go." I turn, but he takes my wrist, stopping me.

"Actually, don't go, I need a distraction." He stands, naked, and pulls me closer. He runs his hands over my shoulders and around my back. "Silk," he murmurs. My mind races with a million different thoughts. This is exactly what happened before . . . and then he crushed me. I step back, ignoring his obvious erection, and he smirks down at me.

"You immune to me now, Bait?"

I give a small, unamused laugh. "Let's not repeat past mistakes, Gunner. It doesn't end well."

"You seeing someone?" he asks, narrowing his eyes.

"None of your business."

"You used to get wet just looking in my direction, Bait. What changed?"

His words disgust me, and I head for the door. "My name is Ava. Your childish nicknames are ridiculous." I leave, slamming his door.

I struggle to get back to sleep. Instead, I lay awake, the night I slept with Gunner playing on my mind like a loop.

The club had been on lockdown, so I was back from university. Gunner was being unusually flirty, and whenever I think back, I always wonder the same thing. Had he decided he was going to have sex with me that night? Was it all set in his mind? He knew he was about to leave for the Army and he'd hardly be around anymore.

Rooster had suggested a drinking game. He was always the one to liven up a party. After who knows how many shots, Gunner and I ended up moving away from everyone else. We sat in the corner of the bar, chatting and being silly. Taking photos with a new filter on my phone that put ridiculous bunny ears on us, we'd laughed like it was the funniest thing in the world.

I'd gone to the toilet, and when I came out, Gunner was waiting in the shadows of the hall. He pulled me into the corner and kissed me like I was his next meal. I remember thinking that I had to make the most of it because he'd pull away any second and realise it was me he was kissing. When he didn't, I got carried away. My heart ran away with my mind, making it all kinds of crazy promises about love and marriage.

He'd taken my hand and led me upstairs to his room. He was the first guy I'd slept with since a couple bad experiences, but I don't remember feeling nervous. To me, Gunner was the guy I was supposed to spend the rest of my life with. I loved him, I always had.

We'd spent the night in each other's arms, and it was the best night of my life. But when he woke the next morning with a look of pure regret plastered on his face, I wanted to scream.

He sat me down to talk, and the way he spoke made me feel like a stupid teenager with a schoolgirl crush. I was mortified and embarrassed, and the amazing night before soon felt wrong and dirty. I'd been used, so when he told me he was heading off to the Army, I was glad. I didn't need him hanging around to witness me falling apart.

I don't sleep for the rest of the night, and Evie decides that five a.m. is the perfect time for us to start the day. "Mummy," she whispers, tapping my face, her hot breath against my cheek.

I open one eye. "Baby it's very early. Can't we have more sleep time?"

She shakes her head and jumps off the bed. I groan. I have work today and it's a twelve-hour shift. How the hell am I going to stay awake? Being a nurse is hard work but add an early-rising child and it's even harder.

We head downstairs, and I settle her in front of the large television in the main room. Because it's so early, there are no brothers hanging around. It's nice and quiet. I make pancakes for Evie and a strong coffee for myself, then I join Evie on the couch. I love these little moments we get alone, even if it is early.

I hum in approval at my first sip of coffee and lay my head back, thinking over all the things I have to do today. The main door opens and Gunner steps inside. He always did love an early morning run. He stops in surprise. "You're up early," he states, moving to grab a bottle of water from the fridge behind the bar.

Evie shuffles behind me out of sight. She's shy with people she doesn't know, and although Gunner's been home twice since she was born, she doesn't remember him.

"The joys of a two-year-old," I joke.

He stops beside the couch, watching Evie, who's now distracted by the pink pig on the television. "She looks like you."

I smile, running my fingers through her soft hair. "Yeah."

"Does she have any of her father's features?" he asks casually.

The biggest question asked, and yet I still won't breathe a word. It's gone on too long now, this burden of a secret. If I thought for one minute that he'd be happy about the news, I'd confess all. But I know he wouldn't, and I don't want to put myself or Evie through that kind of hurt.

"Still a big secret then?" he asks, flopping down in the worn chair opposite where we sit.

"Let's not go there."

Evie pokes her head from around me, her crystal blue eyes watching Gunner closely. "Hey," he smiles, "I bet you don't remember me."

She shakes her head and her long brown hair falls in front of her face. I brush it to one side.

"This is Uncle Dam's best friend, Gunner." Evie struggled to say Damien's name, so he's always been Dam to her, sometimes Dam-dam.

"You're big," she says in a quiet voice.

"I was in the Army, a soldier."

"Was?" I query, and he shrugs, picking at the label on his water bottle. I still sense a story there, but I don't push. He clearly doesn't want to talk about it yet.

"Sorry about last night. Next time, just bang on the bedroom wall and I'll shut up. Sometimes I get dreams, and they mess my head up."

I nod. "Damien was the same when he came home. They don't happen so much now."

Evie gets off the couch and approaches Gunner warily. She holds out her hand and looks at him expectantly. He looks at me, and I nod for him to take her hand, which he does.

She shakes it, just like Damien has taught her to. "I'm Evie and I'm two."

"I'm Gunner and I'm twenty-eight." He turns to me. "She reminds me of you." A smile plays on his lips and, for a second, I think he's happy about that.

I laugh. "Evie's been chatting everyone's head off since she was about fifteen months old. She's quite advanced for two, probably because she's around my mum a lot."

"Your mum, ever the teacher."

My mum left the teaching profession five years ago at the age of fifty. My dad made enough money for them to retire early, and they have an income from various club businesses. Mum spends a lot of time with Evie because of my shift work and she's never been one for baby talk, believing that children learn quicker if spoken to properly. I guess she was right.

"Damien tells me you're still working as a nurse."

"I am. I love it, even though I'm tired all of the time."

"You always wanted to be a nurse . . ." He trails off and then smiles. "I remember you trying to bandage me and Damien up, even when we weren't injured." He laughs, and the sound makes me feel warm inside. I'd forgotten that I love his laugh.

"The good old days," I mutter.

His smile fades. "They were good back then."

The stairs creak under the weight of heavy footfalls and Damien appears, a blonde-haired woman trailing behind him. I roll my eyes. He's always got a woman in his bed, saying it helps with the nightmares he's suffered since his Army days.

"Morning. We didn't wake you, did we?" He grins, swatting the backside of the blonde. She giggles.

"No, not me, brother. I was up and out for a run. Never heard a peep from your room," says Gunner.

I ignore Damien's question. If he'd woken me, he would've known about it. It wouldn't have been the first time I beat the shit out of his door.

CHAPTER TWO

Gunner

I watch Damien as he walks the blonde out, kissing her before saying his goodbyes. What I'd give to have Cameron here right now . . . my balls are bluer than a Smurf's. My attention is brought back to the mini version of Ava, bounding over to Damien and diving into his waiting arms. Man, have things changed since I was last around.

"How's my favourite girl doing?" Damien grins, covering her delicate pale skin in rough kisses. She giggles and stills his head in her tiny hands.

"Stop, Dam. Your face tickles," squeals Evie.

"Are you okay to help Mum watch her while I work today?" Ava's voice sends shivers down my spine. Now, there's a woman who could ease these blue balls.

I've loved Ava since . . . well, I can't even pinpoint a date, it's been so long. We never made anything of it, even though I know she's always felt the same way about me. At first, I stayed away out of respect for Damien and Pops, and then I realised she was destined to be bigger than this MC. She was going places, and I knew if I confessed how I felt, she wouldn't make the most of her potential. Then she finally made it to university, and I knew I'd done the right thing, and so I joined up with the forces, following in the footsteps of Pops and my father, Tank.

Right before I left for the Army, I made the stupid mistake of having one selfish night. I thought if I had one taste, then I could get Ava out of my system and move on. Unfortunately, it didn't work. It made me crave her more, and the next morning, when she woke in my bed with hope and happiness in her eyes, I realised that I'd fucked up. She would have given up everything to be with me, and I didn't want to be responsible for that. So, I forced myself to break her heart. Her hurt eyes have been engraved into my soul forever.

"Hello, Earth to Gunner." Damien's voice brings me back into the room. I realise I'm staring at Ava, and she's looking at me, confusion on her face.

"Sorry, flashbacks," I say as explanation.

"We need to call church, get you up to date on shit. About twelve okay for you?" asks Damien, and I give a nod.

"Well, I'd better get ready for work. Can you watch Evie while I shower?" Ava asks Damien.

He swings the little girl around. "Of course." It suits him, and I wonder why he hasn't taken an ol' lady yet.

I'm still sitting and watching some cartoon about a spoilt little brat of a pig when Ava comes back down the stairs. I do a double take because, fuck, does she look amazing in her uniform. Ava's long brown hair flows down to the curve of her arse in loose curls. Her petite frame makes her B-cup breasts appear bigger than they are, and I smirk at the memory of the tattoo she has under those perfect breasts, one she's never told anyone about. Her tiny waist shows no signs that she had a baby growing in there.

Crouching down, she tucks a stray scrap of hair behind her daughter's tiny ear. "Nan is coming downstairs now to watch you while I go to work. Please be super good for her today, sweetie, because she has one of her headaches."

The little girl nods. "I go to the police." Her cute little words tumble out with excitement.

"The police?" queries Ava.

"Pops said there's an open day at the station. He thinks it'll do her good to respect the police." Damien grins, and we both exchange an amused look.

"No," says Ava. "No, I don't want her around the police."

"Relax, sis, Pops will keep an eye on her."

Ava stands and gives a shrug, a troubled look on her face. "Whatever, it's not like he'll listen to me anyway," she mutters.

At twelve o'clock, I sit to Damien's left at the large oak table, ready for church. Damien bangs the gavel to get everyone's attention. Once it quiets down, he grins and slaps me on the shoulder. "Welcome back, VP. I'm sure I'm not the only one pleased to have you home."

There's a few nods and murmurs of agreement. "I've kept you up to date over the phone whenever possible, but the last few weeks have been hard, brother, I won't lie. There're whispers that the Saints are stepping on our turf. We've put the feelers out, and a few guys from the street have come back with tales of H being pushed on the streets. We don't need this crap, especially with a new chief of police being appointed, part of the reason Pops has gone to the open day today."

"We need to convince the new chief that we can keep our town clean," pipes up Breaker. "That ain't gonna' happen if heroin is doing the rounds right under our nose."

Damien nods. "We need to arrange a meet with their Pres, see what they think they're playing at."

"I say we put a bullet straight through his fuckin' head. Who the hell does he think he is?" growls Maddocks.

I nod in agreement. "Let's handle it old school."

"Nah, times have changed. We're doing good at straightening shit out. We just gotta get a hold on it, that's all. If they don't back off, then we'll look at other ways around it," says Damien firmly. "Let's vote. Everyone in favour of calling a meet?" It's a unanimous vote, and the conversation moves to more relaxed topics.

"No ol' lady, Gunner?" asks Rooster.

"Not yet, Roost, though there's someone special, Cammie. How's Gemma?"

His eyes light up, and I feel that pang of jealousy that he's sorted with his wife and kid and I'm still sorting my shit out. "Man, she's amazing. Best thing I ever did was claim her."

"Cammie is coming over later. You'll have to introduce her to Gemma," I suggest.

The other guys move out, but Damien and I remain. "Cammie is coming here?" he asks, grabbing a bottle of whisky from the cabinet to his right. He pours us each a finger of the amber liquid and sits back down.

"Yeah, she wants to meet the guys," I say.

"So, she's someone then, not just a fling?"

I met Cammie six months ago on a night out with the Army lads. She had the most amazing little black dress on that clung to every curve, and her long tanned legs had me hooked. Once I got them wrapped around me, I decided I wasn't going to let this one go easily. Lucky for me, she felt the same, and even though it's been hard with me being in the Army, she's been very patient, dropping things to fit me in when I've had last-minute leave and travelling to see me.

"I'm seeing where it goes. Things are just better when she's around."

He grins, taking a sip of his drink. "Does Ava know?"

It isn't a secret that Ava's had a thing for me since she was a teenager, and the brothers often make jokes about it. These days, I think those feelings have passed. She seems happy and content with her life, and I don't notice the longing in her eyes like before. I treated her badly after our one night together, so the fact she even bothers to talk to me is a blessing.

"Brother, let it go. Ava doesn't feel like that anymore. She's grown, had a kid. It was a silly teenage crush."

He shrugs. "I still like to give her shit for it, though. She keeps talking about some arsehole doctor who won't leave her alone. Whenever she dates those fuckers, I like to mention you in the hope it puts them off."

I clench my fists under the table. The thought of her with someone else does something to my chest. Maybe I'm not as relaxed about being around her as I thought I would be. "She seeing him?"

He shakes his head. "Nope, she goes on the odd date, but she's pretty busy with Evie and work. I sometimes think she's still pining after the fucker who got her pregnant." He knocks back the rest of his drink, anger clouding his face.

It was a dark time for me when I discovered Ava had a kid. I know the rest of the club had been shocked too, but they kept that shit from me, so I didn't lose focus in Afghanistan. She hadn't been dating anyone that we knew of, but she was away at Uni, so Damien assumed she kept it quiet. But still to this day, she doesn't talk about Evelyn's dad. Every time I think about that fucker leaving her to bring up the baby alone, it makes me want to hunt him down and beat the shit outta him. But I guess every guy in the club wants blood for that fuck-up.

"The kid's cute. She reminds me of Ava when she was small."

Damien smiles, rubbing the bristles on his chin. "Ava's an amazing mum, and Evie is the princess around here, exactly like Ava was when she was a kid." Damien's right—Ava was the princess from the day she was born. I remember, at four years old, peeking into her crib and poking her. Pops told me that Damien and I were gonna protect her like she was the most precious diamond in the world for the rest of our lives, I guess we both felt like we'd let him down when she got pregnant.

It's almost eight in the evening when Cammie finally calls me to say she's outside. I rush out and pull her into my arms, lifting her so she can wrap those long legs around my hips. I press her against her car, kissing her like she's my last meal.

"Wow, you missed me, big guy?" she asks, grinning.

I press my face into her warm neck, taking in her perfect scent of freshness and strawberries.

"You have no idea," I mumble into her blonde curls. I set her down, taking her hand. "Come and meet the guys, then we can get to the good part."

We're greeted at the door by Damien holding a sleepy Evie. "Good to finally meet you, Cammie. He's been like a lovesick puppy dog all day, waiting at the window."

I scowl at him and thump him on the arm. "This is Damien, my Pres."

Cammie smiles and shakes his hand. "And who's this little cutie?"

"This is my niece, Evelyn. She's waiting up to give a kiss to her mummy, who should be here any minute," explains Damien. "Could you just take her a second, Gunner? I need to take a piss."

I shrug uncomfortably, but Damien doesn't seem to notice and places her in my arms. Evie doesn't seem to mind because she rests her head on my shoulder.

Cammie smiles. "Wow, suits you," she says with a wink.

"Don't get no ideas, lady. I want you to myself for a long while yet."

"Mummy," shrieks Evie suddenly, sitting herself up in my arms.

I look to the window to see Ava step out of Maddocks' car. My heart beats a little faster, partly because I feel like she won't want me holding her daughter and because I'm nervous about introducing Cammie to her. It's important to me that they get along. I've known Ava a long time, her whole life, and despite our past, I want her to like Cammie.

Ava steps inside, shrugging out of her cardigan, and I admire how gorgeous she looks even though she's just done a twelve-hour shift. She stops when she sees me with Evie and her eyes fall to Cammie, who's holding onto my arm.

"What are you still doing up, little one?" she asks.

"I missed you. Uncle Dam said I could wait."

Ava reaches for her, taking her out of my arms and sitting her on her hip. She places random kisses over her face, making Evie giggle.

"Ava, this is Cameron," I announce, bringing her attention back to me.

"Call me Cammie." She smiles politely, holding out her hand towards Ava.

Ava eyes it for a second before taking it firmly. "Ava, Damien's sister."

"From what Ash tells me, you're more than just Damien's sister. You all grew up together?"

"Ash?" repeats Ava, looking to me. It isn't very often anyone uses my first name, apart from my mother and now Cammie. It must sound foreign to Ava.

"I can't have her calling me Gunner. She's my girl." I grin, kissing the side of Cammie's head. Ava narrows her eyes. I don't know why I had to make a point of saying that. It's pretty obvious seeing as she's the first woman I've ever introduced to the club.

Damien re-joins us, kissing Ava on the head in greeting. "How about I put Evie to bed and we all sit down for a drink to make Cammie feel welcome?"

Ava shakes her head. "I'm tired after that shift, so I'm just going to hit the sack. It was nice to meet you, Cammie. Goodnight."

I watch as she disappears. "I don't think she likes me. Do you two have history?" whispers Cammie.

I laugh, trying to hide the lie that's about to fall from my mouth. "No way. She's like a sister to me. She's just being protective, I guess."

After a few drinks and a catch-up with Damien, we make our excuses and I drag Cammie towards my room. She closes the door, and I have her against it within seconds.

"Easy, Gunner," she teases. She hates my road name.

I pull her top over her head and then unbutton her jeans. "Get them off. I need skin, baby."

Once she's down to her underwear, I take a step back, taking a mental picture of the pink lace garments that stand between us.

Cammie reaches for my belt, slowly unfastening it and bending to her knees. "How many of those women downstairs have you fucked?" She's referring to the club girls who hang around purely to have sex with the guys. Not any one in particular, just whoever wants them.

Cammie slides the belt from my jeans and hands it to me. I watch as she pulls at the buttons and then fights to get the denim over my hips.

"I don't know a lot of the club girls now, most of them are new," I say.

"But you slept with club girls before?" I nod, sucking in a breath as she pulls my hard shaft from my boxers. "Did they suck your cock as good as me?"

"Remind me how good you are and I'll let you know."

Cammie grins up at me and then runs the tip of her tongue over the head of my cock. I grip the belt tighter as she slides me into her mouth. She takes half my shaft before I hit the back of her throat. "You want me to use the belt?" I ask, and she nods, sucking my cock deeper into her throat. I hold the buckle end and swing the leather down towards her arse, catching it enough to make her tense. She sucks harder, and I grip a hand in her hair. "Fuck," I groan as she gags against the intrusion. It's another minute before I pull away from her. "If you keep doing that, I'm gonna come, and I need to be inside you."

Cammie stands, wiping her mouth on the back of her hand. There's something sexy about it, and I take a few deep breaths to calm myself. She bends over the bed with her arse in the air, ready for the belt. Cammie loves to play rough. I pull the pink knickers down to her knees and step to the side. "Five?" I ask, and she gives a nod, pressing her face to the quilt.

I bring the belt down hard against her perfect arse, and she lets out a yelp. I rub my cock. The red mark on her skin makes me want to fuck her hard, but I promised her five, so I carry on, bringing the leather down one after the other. The thwack of the belt makes her tense each time, gripping the sheets up into her delicate, tight fists.

I drop the belt and position myself behind her, leaving her knickers around her knees. I push into her, pausing halfway to give her a chance to adjust. By the time I'm fully in, she's moaning and squirming against me, almost ready to come. I begin to move, slow at first before picking up a punishing pace. She grips the headboard to give herself more leverage as I ram in to her. I recognise the keening sound she begins to make, it's the tell-tale sign that she's going to orgasm and I reach around to pinch her nipples, causing her to scream out my name as she shudders around my cock.

There's a thudding against the bedroom wall and we both freeze, Cammie still breathing hard as the final shudders rip through her body. I realise the banging is coming from Ava's room. We must have woken her. Knowing Ava can hear me gets me harder, and I begin to move again. Ava's crazy if she thinks I'm gonna stop before I've had my release.

I wrap Cammie's hair around my large fist and push into her hard, making sure I'm fully in each time before pulling out and pushing back in. I'm groaning loud enough to earn another bang on the wall from Ava.

"Jesus, Ashton," pants Cammie, looking over her shoulder at me with a satisfied grin, "I think you've upset your neighbour."

"I ain't been inside you for too long baby, I ain't stopping until I've filled you with my—" I stop when there's an angry banging on the door. "Fuck," I huff, pulling out and grabbing a T-shirt. I wipe my cock with it and grab my boxers from the floor, pulling them on and ripping the door open.

"What the fuck is your problem?" I growl.

Ava takes a step back and looks me up and down, her chest heaving with rage. "Some of us are trying to sleep. Some of us have been at work for the last twelve hours."

"Well, some of us need to fuck. Maybe if you did that, you wouldn't be so uptight," I grate out.

"I fuck quietly, so I don't wake the rest of the club," she retorts.

That comment pisses me off and I make a note to ask Damien if she brings guys back here. "Bait, I don't believe you. Prudes don't fuck, they make love," I say, using air quotation marks to exaggerate the 'make love' part.

"We both know that's not true, Ashton." Ava arches an eyebrow. I don't want Cammie to hear if she's going to go down that road, so I step out into the hall and close my bedroom door.

"Don't ever bring that up again, Ava. It was three years ago, and I was wasted on shots. I regret every second of it and I don't want Cammie to know."

"I don't want anyone to know our dirty little secret either, but don't make out I'm being a prude. You're keeping me awake, and I have a child in there. It's unfair."

I watch her head back to her room, her T-shirt barely covering her perky little backside. I'm hard again and I groan, pushing my door open. Cammie is fast asleep. I look down at the bulge in my boxers. Fuck Ava and her whining. It's gonna be a long night.

CHAPTER THREE

Ava

I stare at the ceiling, seething. The noises from next door are still going on, and I couldn't sleep now even if I wanted to. I actually think he's doing it on purpose just to piss me off.

The fact I've not had sex in at least three months is not helping my frustrations. I hear a scream followed by Gunner's growl. That's at least the fourth time I've heard him come, he's like a machine.

It goes silent and I pray they're finally getting some sleep, because lord knows I need it. I snuggle against Evie, who hasn't stirred once. I think an earthquake could rock the building and she'd still sleep.

By the morning, I haven't cooled off any, so I decide to get out of the clubhouse before I have to see Gunner and his new piece of arse slobbering all over each other. I'm moody from lack of sleep, and the last thing I need is the visual of them put together with the sound effects from last night.

Emma is just opening up her café bar, Emzie's, when Evie and I turn up. I give her a hug and then help her take the chairs from the tables while Evie plays with her dolls at her favourite table by the window.

"How is it having Gunner back?" asks Emma, switching on the coffee machine.

"Don't even mention him, Em. He kept me awake most of the night last night, and I'm exhausted."

She eyes me suspiciously. "Am I missing something?"

"God, no, I meant he kept me awake with his noise while he banged his new wifey."

"New wifey? He's taken an ol' lady?"

I shrug, pulling up a stool to the bar and sitting down. Emma pours two coffees and sits next to me. "She must be important cos he introduced her to the club last night." I sigh.

Emma strokes my arm gently, a look of sympathy on her face. "That's pretty shitty for you."

She knows all about me and Gunner and our one night together. She and Chloe have been my best friends since our teen years, and they knew all about my crush because Gunner was all I ever talked about.

"I'm so over him, Emma. It's been years. It was a shock to see him, and then to meet her, but I'm fine with it."

She gives me a knowing look. "You don't need to pretend to me, Ava, I know you."

The door chimes, indicating a customer, and we both turn as Maddocks walks in. His smouldering glare would melt the panties off the most immune woman. His large frame, dark skin, and brown eyes have an effect on the majority of women at the club, even me. Not that I'd go there, of course, because he and Emma have a love-hate relationship that borders on insane. Neither will commit but the sex is intense, or so I'm told. Emma makes my toes curl with her stories.

"You didn't hear me knocking at your door last night?" his voice rumbles, making Emma and I exchange a cautious look.

"Shall I just . . ." I go to get up, but Emma shakes her head and holds onto my arm until I lower back onto the stool.

"I heard you. Half the street heard you. I just wasn't in the mood for you last night," says Emma, a hint of annoyance in her tight smile.

Maddocks removes the shades perched on the top of his head, arching an eyebrow at her. "I'm sorry?" He's daring her to repeat it, and I pray she doesn't. I've been around some of their arguments and I often wonder how she isn't intimidated by Maddocks. The guys call him 'Mad' for short, and the nickname suits him perfectly. Being the Enforcer for the club is a nasty job, one that requires a hard face and an even harder heart. I've heard stories of his no-mercy attitude.

"I was tired, and I'd been on the phone with . . ." She pauses for effect, and I cringe. Please tell me she isn't trying to make him jealous. "It doesn't matter, you don't know him."

I groan, placing my head in my hands. I feel the heat radiating from Maddocks as anger surges through his veins. "This cos of Layla?" he grits out.

"Who?" she asks innocently, taking a sip of coffee.

"We ain't together, I can fuck who I want." His sudden tone of anger makes me jump, and I glance to Evie, who's still playing with her dolls, unaware of the shitstorm around us.

"I know, you keep telling me. So, I rang someone who wants to be with me, just me, no club girls."

"Who?" he growls.

"You don't know him. He's a nice guy, owns a bar up town. He's been asking me out for ages, but I was busy wasting my time with you."

"I'll smash every fuckin' bar in town if I have to. You ain't seeing him."

"I am—we're going on a date. Imagine that, Maddocks, an actual date, something you've never done."

"I don't do dates, Emma," he growls.

"He does. I'm excited, so don't ruin it for me."

Maddocks snarls in frustration. "I'm following you." And then he goes and sits at the table next to Evie, chatting away to her like none of this just happened.

I gasp. "Oh my god, he's literally going to stay here all day and follow you everywhere."

"He'll get called for a run soon enough. He's never around for more than a few hours," she says, not looking worried at all.

"Have you really called someone else?"

Emma nods. "I was going to ask you to come with me. He's got a friend, and Chloe is driving me insane with her crying over Darren. I need a normal human to come with me."

"What, to have Maddocks accuse me of taking sides? He'll make my life hell at the club."

"He won't even know. Trust me, he'll go soon. The date's tonight at nine. Come. It's about time you got some action of your own. You'll only be listening to Gunner all night again."

I groan, but she's right, so I agree.

It's half-past nine in the evening and I'm sitting at a table in a French restaurant. The two guys opposite me and Emma are nice-looking but not in a way that would usually turn my head. My guy, Jonathon, is twenty-six and a medical student, wanting to become a surgeon. Emma's guy, the bar owner, is called Mark and he's twenty-eight. They both play rugby, but they aren't built like Gunner or Maddocks.

"So, you're free and single?" Jonathon asks, leaning in close to me.

I give a nod. "Yeah, sort of. I mean, I'm not in a relationship, but I have a protective family, which can make my dating life difficult sometimes."

Jonathon laughs. "I always win the hearts of mums and nans, don't worry."

"They don't get much of a say in my family, unfortunately. I have a lot of brothers."

He shrugs, seemingly unfazed. "I like a challenge. I can win them over, I'm sure. Do they play rugby by any chance?"

The thought of some of the Eagles playing any kind of sport makes me laugh. "God, no, sports is not something they do a lot of."

We spend some time making polite conversation and then Emma suggests moving on to Morrell's, a bar just up from the club. I wait for her to excuse herself for the bathroom and follow her. "Emma, what are you playing at? You know taking these guys to Morrell's will cause trouble."

"Maddocks won't be there," she says innocently. She's right, he won't be because the clubhouse has its own bar, but there will be eyes who will get him there in minutes.

"Maddocks will come, and then what? You're gonna get this guy beat up and he hasn't done anything wrong."

"Don't be so dramatic. Maddocks won't do anything to him. The most he'll do is glare at me across the room until I cave. Well, guess what, I'm not going to tonight. I'm sick of catching him pawing at the club girls like there's one rule for him and another for me. I'm not his personal whore."

I realise Emma has a point and I start to feel bad for her. Plus, I've had a bottle of wine, so I'm feeling brave. Damien always tells me to drink at the bars nearer the club because it's easier for him to get eyes on me, so at least I'll please him for once.

We arrive at Morrell's by taxicab half an hour later. The bar is busy, and I notice a few of the Eagles prospects straight away. They watch me closely, not looking happy about Jonathon, who doesn't leave my side. It takes a full five minutes before Maddocks swaggers into the bar, his shades firmly in place. I wonder if he can see a damn thing with them on in here.

He heads over to me, leaning in close to my ear. "Where is she?"

"Maddocks, don't even bother to play the game. She wants a reaction."

He grins, lifting his shades and eyeing Jonathon with amusement. "This what you came out for, Ava?"

I roll my eyes. "I'm doing Em a favour."

Jonathon holds his hand out to Maddocks, who stares at it coldly. "Hi, I'm Jon."

I inwardly groan. "Be nice," I mutter to Maddocks. He doesn't shake Jonathon's hand, so Jonathon retracts it. "You are?"

"About to get real pissed if I don't find your friend soon. I take it he's with my girl?"

"He went out back with Ava's friend," says Jonathon innocently. "She said she was single."

"She fuckin' lied," growls Maddocks. I groan again, and before I can stop him, Maddocks is making his way through the crowd.

"He was intense," says Jonathan, bringing my attention back to him.

I sigh. "Yeah, one of the brothers I was telling you about."

He looks confused. "But he's black," he states.

I nod. "Yes, I'd noticed," I say, not wanting to elaborate. His comment narks me. In this day and age, it's wrong to assume that Maddocks and I couldn't possibly be related because of our skin colour.

I knock back a shot. I don't have to pay in this bar, thanks to my status with The Eagles MC.

"I need to dance," I say, making my way towards the small dance floor, not caring if Jonathon follows me or not.

Unfortunately, he does, deciding to dance close to me, his hands all over my arse. I grit my teeth, but at least I'm not alone for once. Maybe I should take a page from Emma's book and use Jonathon to keep Gunner awake tonight, although somehow I don't think Jonathon is the type to growl and throw me around the room. I giggle at the thought.

I wrap my arms around Jonathon's neck. Maybe if I kiss him, it'll light a spark, so I lean up and gently plant my lips on his. It's a nice, calm kiss, which disappoints me. I was hoping it would be all teeth and passion. He smiles down at me as we continue to move to the music.

Glancing to my left, I stare straight into the stormy green eyes of Gunner. It surprises me and catches me off guard. This isn't the kind of bar I'd expect Gunner to drink in. His jaw is ticking, a sign he's clenching his teeth, and I inwardly kick myself for knowing this intimate detail about him.

Jonathon snuggles into my neck, kissing gently along my skin. My eyes are still locked on Gunner, whose eyebrows raise at Jonathon's bold move. Suddenly, there's a tap on my shoulder and Grill smiles down at me. That smile tells me all I need to know—they're gonna cockblock me.

"Really, Ava? So, you just leave my daughter with anyone who'll have her and fuck off to some dead-end bar?" snaps Grill, his anger convincing to anyone who doesn't know him.

Jonathon takes a step back, confused by the large guy glaring at me. "Get stuffed, Grill, that's not funny." I turn to Jonathon. "He's kidding," I say.

"No, you're damn right it ain't funny. If you weren't my baby mama, I'd kick your arse for being such a whore. You don't care about anyone but yourself."

I roll my eyes. "Seriously, Jonathon, I'm really sorry about this. This arsehole is another of my brothers."

"Yea, she tells you she has a complicated family, loads of brothers. She'll introduce you to her three kids—all by different dads, by the way—and you'll be uncle number eighty-odd. Trust me, mate, I'm doing you a favour when I say run."

Grill takes my hand and pulls me towards Gunner, who sits back, a smug look on his annoyingly handsome face. "Thanks a lot, Grill. Don't you guys ever get fed up of babysitting me?" I huff.

I lower into the chair opposite Gunner. "You can do better," he says, eyeing Jonathon, who's now chatting to another girl.

"I don't get a chance because one of you guys always turn up. Don't you want me to be happy?"

Gunner fiddles with his cigarette packet, turning it over and over in his hand. "Do you honestly think you'd be happy with a normal guy like that? He'll give you the house and babies, but will he give you the Earth-shattering orgasms?"

I blush. "I want the house and babies. Orgasms aren't everything."

"Orgasms are everything. That's the reason you're such a miserable bitch," he mutters.

I'm offended by his judgement. He's been back two minutes and has made that assumption already.

"It's because I'm so tired all the time," I argue. "Where's Cameron, by the way?"

"Out with her friends."

I note he doesn't look happy about this. Being the control freak he is, I'm surprised he allowed it. "So, go and babysit her," I suggest.

"Damien put me on you, and I trust Cammie."

I roll my eyes, sickness filling my stomach. I hate that he seems so loved-up with her. I never had to go through this before because Gunner's never been serious enough about a woman to bring her home to meet everyone.

I stand suddenly, realising too late that the sickness is making its way up my throat and into my mouth. I dash towards the door, footsteps thundering after me. Flinging open the bar door, I run out into the carpark and bend over, resting my hands on my knees, I empty the entire contents of my stomach onto the ground.

"Fucking hell," groans Grill, turning away from the scene before him, and I close my eyes. I know without looking that every Eagles member from inside this bar will be behind me, even if most of them are just prospects.

I risk a glance behind me and find six guys, all watching me, Gunner at the front. He grins and then starts to laugh. This sets everyone else off. I wipe my mouth on the back of my hand and stand up straight. "Yeah, yeah, very funny," I mutter, humiliation spreading through me. "Which one of you clowns can take me home?"

CHAPTER FOUR

Gunner

I hold out a napkin to Ava, so she can wipe herself down. My heart is still pumping fast. For a second, I thought something bad was about to happen. The way she dived up scared the crap out of me.

I hold my bike keys up. "I'll take you now."

Ava hesitates, looking around at the other guys like she's trying to weigh up her options. She knows damn well these fuckers aren't going to offer her a lift home now that I have.

We all turn to the sudden commotion that is Maddocks and Emma. He's walking from the bar like he hasn't got a care in the world, a smug look on his face. Emma is screaming and shouting at his back, waving her arms around like a crazy person.

"And you think I'm your property? Well, I'm not! You want me at your beck and call, then you put me on the back of your bike for real," she screams.

Maddocks waltzes over to his ride, swinging his leg over and pulling on his helmet. He starts the engine, and Ava sees her chance, running over and jumping on the bike.

"Can I grab a lift?" she asks, avoiding looking at me.

I can't make a big deal about it, she knows I can't. Maddocks would question why I'm so desperate to have her on my bike, and what would I say without giving the game away? That I want to feel her heat at my back? That would definitely raise some unwanted questions.

Maddocks passes his spare helmet back to Ava, and she puts it on. "Gunner, you're okay to take Emma home, aren't you?" she asks me.

I give her a smile, one full of promise that I'll get her back for this. "No problems at all, Bait."

I watch as she wraps her slender arms around Maddocks, her thighs pressing against the outside of his, and I have to look away before I rip her from the bike and drag her with me.

By the time I get to the clubhouse, the place is packed out. I can't get used to all these people and the noise of the juke box constantly throwing out some trashy song. I grab a beer from Tap at the bar and take a seat in a dark corner, checking my phone for the hundredth time to make sure Cammie hasn't messaged me for a pick-up. She hasn't.

When I look up from the phone, Ava is in the arms of Jackson. He's from one of our other charters and stops by whenever he's on a run this way. I like Jackson, but I'm not sure I like the way he's looking down at Ava like she's on the menu. I pick at the beer mat, catching every smile she gives him and every touch he places on her.

I look around to see if Damien is seeing this shit and notice him watching me. He heads over and sits opposite. "You okay, Gunner?"

I give a nod and tip my beer back, wincing at the bitter taste. "I'm good, D. Why wouldn't I be?"

"You look pissed as hell. You stressed about Cammie being out?" he queries.

I shrug. That would be the easiest explanation, but I know I'm not. Sure, I'd prefer if Cammie was here to distract me from a certain brunette, but I can't tell Damien that.

"Cammie isn't the kind of girl you can tell to stay home. I'm fine with it, though. What about you? I don't see no ol' lady on the horizon."

He smirks. "I can't give up the constant flow of pussy. I like it too much."

"I hear Chloe is single now," I point out.

Damien almost chokes on his beer, coughing and spluttering before wiping his mouth and eyeing me like I've lost my mind. It's all a front. I know he loves that girl. He has since the day she came home with Ava, looking all vulnerable and sad.

It was Ava's third year in secondary school and Chloe had joined that day. Ava always befriended the new kids or the outcasts, it's in her nature to be kind. Chloe was a puzzle to Damien. Her parents were always out and about, socializing at charity events, leaving her home alone, and she never seemed to be happy. Their huge mansion and the fact that they were rich didn't faze Chloe. She wasn't interested in material things. Chloe loved Ava's life, thought she was lucky to have all the guys looking after her, and she soon became a permanent fixture around the club, even getting her own room for when she wanted to stop over.

Damien never made a move on Chloe, but I know he wanted to. Things just never happened for them, either he had too much shit going down with the club or she was at university or in a relationship. Once he became President, he got too absorbed in the biker lifestyle, with pussy on tap and runs for days on end. "What the hell's that got to do with me finding an ol' lady?" he asks.

"Come on, D, I saw the way you were with her. Even the other night when she was here, you couldn't take your eyes off her."

"What, like you and my sister?"

I clench my jaw. "I can't help if your sister had a thing for me."

"Like those feelings were never mutual. Do you think I walk around with my head up my arse?"

"Forget it, I was just pointing out that Chloe was single. Obviously, I got it wrong, there's nothing there between you," I huff. "Any news from the Saints? There was no unusual activity at Morrell's." Another reason I was at the bar when Ava was there.

"Their Pres agreed to a meet on Friday, but I feel like something's off. I've got Sneak on them, watching, but he's not reported anything suspicious yet."

"Maybe they were just pushing their luck, and now they know you've clicked on to them, they'll back the fuck off?"

A text comes through on my mobile. It's Cammie telling me she's at her friend's house and she's had a great night. It pisses me off that she didn't come back here—I need some action. Since coming back from Afghanistan, sex is all I can think about. I'd quite happily spend the day inside any pussy right now.

I rub my hands across my tired face. "If there're any runs coming up, send me. I need to get out of here for a few days." Damien eyes me, concern on his face, but he gives a nod in acknowledgment.

I look in Ava's direction, and she's dancing against Jackson, his hands clung to her hips. "You letting this shit slide?"

Damien follows my eyeline. "Jackson is alright. I think he and Ava had a thing a few months ago. She's twenty-four now, man, I can't control her the way I used to." He laughs, shaking his head. "The sooner she settles down, the happier I'll be, so I can stop stressing about her."

"You always said you didn't want her settling for a biker."

"But she never left this life. Even when she got pregnant, she stuck around. I don't think she'd be happy out of this life with some nine-to-five guy," he says.

"Do you still think Evie's father is one of us?" I ask, knocking the rest of my beer back.

"She tells me not, says he's some waste of space who was just in town for some training course for his job. Reckons he's long gone and knows nothing about the kid."

"I still can't believe she ended up pregnant. Ava's not someone I'd ever thought to be that dumb," I say, shaking my head.

"It worked out for the best. Ava was messed up for a short time back then. Getting pregnant sorted her head out. She stepped up and she does good by that little girl. She's a great mum."

"Messed up?" I repeat.

Damien nods. "Yeah, not sure what happened, but there were a few months where all she did was party and get drunk, like she was trying to block something out. Even Pops was worried about her. We thought she was having flashbacks of that night, so Pops tried her at therapy again, but she went once and then refused to go again."

I clench my jaw, realising Ava may have gone off the rails because of me. It was nothing to do with flashbacks. The way I left her cut her up, it was obvious from the look in her eyes when I purposely broke her heart. If I could change that day, I would. I never would have gone there. It was selfish.

I watch as she wraps her arms around Jackson's neck. He's a big guy, and she has to stand on her tiptoes to reach him. He lowers his head slightly, smiling, and then they kiss. It's a full-on, tongue-swiping kiss, and I ball my fists under the table.

"Fuck, Jackson, take the porn show out of my face, would yah," I yell, turning the heads of a few of the guys. Damien smirks at me but say's nothing.

"Sorry, VP, can't control myself round this one." Jackson grins, and I contemplate ramming my fist into his face. Ava is chewing on her bottom lip, her eyes full of lust and want.

I stand abruptly. "Get me a decent club girl, D. I need to make up for lost time," I grate out. Damien shouts over to a brunette. "No, not brunette," I say quickly. "A blonde." I can't have anyone who reminds me of Ava, it's too distracting.

He frowns and then calls over Mina, a tall blonde with a sexy smile. "What about Cammie?" asks Damien.

"She should've been here," I snap, taking Mina's hand and pulling her to me.

I take her out back, which is not normally my style, but I can't have her in my room. I unbuckle my jeans, and she's already on her knees, knowing what's expected of her. I hand her a condom, and she expertly rolls it over my shaft. I might need a release, but I don't trust any of these girls, even though I know Damien pays for them to get checked regularly. Her mouth works me like a pro, but it doesn't stop the rage flowing through me at seeing Ava and Jackson kissing. I take a deep breath, trying to concentrate on how good this girl's mouth feels on my cock. I don't even know why I'm letting Ava get under my skin, it's not like we like each other anymore.

My mind wanders to Ava and that night I spent worshipping her. The feel of her warm body under me, and the way she moaned my name when I ate her pussy. The sweetest-tasting girl I've ever had.

I grip Mina's head, holding her still with my cock halfway down her throat. I come on a roar while she gags, trying to push me away. I release her, and she falls back. "Sorry, I got carried away," I say, offering her my hand and pulling her to her feet.

"That's okay. Want me to keep you company tonight?"

I fasten my jeans, shaking my head. "Not tonight."

Needing a shower, I get to my room and grab my towel and wash bag. Guilt is beginning to set in over the blowjob, and I know Cammie will have my balls if she finds out.

I head for the shared bathroom on this floor. We each have a small washroom with a sink and toilet in our room, but the shower and bath are in a separate room.

I swing the door open and freeze. Steam billows out, leaving me face to face with Ava, who's naked and wet, her face flushed. Jackson has her legs wrapped around his waist and he's thrusting into her and moaning into her neck.

"Are you fucking serious?" I bellow. Ava jumps in fright, looking in my direction. They were so lost in bliss, they didn't even hear me come in.

"Jesus, Gunner, what's your problem?" Jackson grabs a towel and covers Ava's breasts. *Too late, fucker, I've already seen them*, I think angrily.

"What's wrong with your room?" I hiss at Ava.

"Evie," she snaps, looking furious.

"I'll give you a knock when we're done," Jackson says, glaring at me.

"I need a shower," I say, leaning against the doorway. It's a shit move, but I'm pissed and I want him gone.

"Get out, Gunner," orders Ava, frustration apparent on her face.

"Man, I ain't finished yet. If you don't get the fuck out, I'll carry on with you watching," warns Jackson. I feel the red mist descending over me like a blanket, and it only takes two steps for me to reach him. I shove him, and he falls away from Ava, who lets out a surprised scream.

"Who the fuck do you think you're talking to? Are you forgetting who the fuck I am?" I roar.

Jackson holds his hands up, trying to get out an apology, but I'm too far gone to stop now. I ram my fist into his smug face, satisfaction beginning to settle in my gut. "I'm your VP, so if I tell you to get the fuck out, you get the fuck out."

I feel a tug on my arm and shrug it away, turning back to see Ava falling to the floor, the towel coming loose from her body. She lands with a thud, catching the back of her head on the sink unit.

"Shit, Ava, are you okay?" I rush to her, crouching by her side. Tears glisten in her eyes, and she shuffles back away from me. "Don't do that," I sigh, "you're not scared of me."

"I don't even know you right now," she mutters, placing her hand to the back of her head and pulling it away with blood on her fingertips.

"Fuck, let me see," I groan, shuffling around her. There's a small cut on her head, nothing major, but I press a towel to it anyway. Jackson is watching us. "Get the hell out of here now," I shout.

"I'm really sorry, Jackson. I'll call you tomorrow," says Ava.

"No, you won't. You stay the fuck away from Ava, and that's a direct order," I warn. Jackson looks pissed but knows better than to argue.

Once he's gone, I pass Ava my towel, and she wraps it around herself. "Get a shower," I order. "I'll wait here."

She glares at me. "I'm not having a shower with you in the same room."

"You don't have a choice. I can't leave you when you've just banged your head, and you need to wash that prick from you." Her cheeks turn red, and I can't tell if it's anger or embarrassment.

"Jackson," I huff, "really, Ava? You can do better." I help her get to her feet.

"It's nothing to do with you, Gunner. You can't just come back after years of being gone and start bossing me around. I don't belong to you or anyone else. I'm not doing anything wrong." She steps into the shower, pulling the curtain between us.

"You're worth more than a quick fuck," I growl.

She laughs, but it's empty. "Really? Shall we talk about what happened three years ago, Gunner? Because that wasn't romance and relationships, was it? I seem to remember it being a cheap fuck. And if you'd been around lately, you'd realise Jackson and I are more than friends. We hook up regular."

I rip the shower curtain back, anger pulsing through me again. She spins around, shocked, wrapping her arms over her the body parts she wants to hide from me. "That shit stops now," I growl, balling my hands to fists. "And stop covering yourself up. I've seen it all before."

"I actually hate you right now. Get out of here," she snaps.

"Not a chance, Bait. You might have a concussion and that's on me, so I'm watching you tonight." It was a small bump, but right now, I'm looking for any excuse to be around her.

Ava's eyes widen. "No, you're not. I'm a nurse, and I know the signs to watch out for." She turns the shower off, and I reach in, turning it back on. "What are you doing?" she screeches, moving out of the jet spray and standing in the far corner of the shower.

I shove my jeans down my legs and pull off my T-shirt. Ignoring the fact that I'm semi-hard, I step under the spray. "Don't move an inch, Bait."

She remains in the corner of the shower, but I know I'm affecting her because I can hear her heavy breathing. I ignore her, washing down my body like she isn't watching me. "You are so out of order right now," she almost whispers.

"I'm keeping the club princess safe." She hates that term, and I know it'll piss her off even more.

Once I've rinsed myself, I turn the water off and grab two towels, chucking one in her direction. She watches as I move around the bathroom, picking up her scattered clothes.

"When are you going back?" she asks, referring to the Army. I'm not ready to tell her I'm done with it, so I ignore her and press the pile of clothes into her arms. I shove her in front as we leave the bathroom, pushing her towards my room. She lets me guide her inside and watches while I pull on some shorts. Then I move her back to her room, but she stops outside the door. "What are you doing? You can't come in, Evie is asleep," she protests. Ignoring her, I twist the handle and we quietly go inside.

Evie is spread out on the bed, looking peaceful and cute. I smile. Grabbing a blanket from the end of the bed, I sit in the leather armchair in the corner of the bedroom as Ava watches me, chewing on that lower lip. "Tell me about the Army, Gunner. Why aren't you going back?" she whispers.

I pull the blanket over me. "Tell me about Evie's father, Ava, and I'll tell you about the Army."

She rolls her eyes. "Old news, Gunner, change the record."

Ava pulls a T-shirt over her head and drops the towel as the shirt lowers. I make no secret that I'm checking out her golden legs. I'm a leg man, and Ava's are perfect. She gently gets into bed, not disturbing Evie. "You can't sleep in the chair all night," she whispers.

I grin. "Is that an offer to join you in the bed?"

"Definitely not. That ship sailed a long time ago."

"I've slept standing up, so the chair is comfort."

That's the last sentence I remember before drifting off to sleep.

I open one eye to find the mini version of Ava sitting on my knee, looking at me with interest. "Morning, little one," I whisper, noting Ava is still fast asleep.

"Why are you in here?" she asks, tilting her pretty little head to one side.

"Me and your mummy were talking. I must have fallen asleep. Shall we go and get some breakfast, let your mummy have some rest?" I suggest.

She smiles and nods, grabbing my hand and leading me from the room eagerly.

CHAPTER FIVE

Ava

I stretch out and yawn, moving= my hand to the side of me to feel around for Evie. When the only thing by my side is empty space and cold sheets, I sit up quickly, looking around. Evie always wakes me. I grab my mobile to check the time and see it's ten in the morning. I've never slept past seven. My heart hammers in my chest, and I dive out of bed, pulling on some leggings as I rush down the stairs.

Evie is sitting on Gunner's shoulders while he chats happily to a few of the guys. He looks at ease with her and it twists my heart. When he sees me, he offers a small smile, which I don't return. "How's the head?" he asks.

"Why didn't you wake me?"

"We went to Macdoodles," announces Evie happily.

"It's McDonald's, sweetie," I correct her. "That was a nice treat." Tap places a fresh coffee on the bar for me, and I take it gratefully.

"What are your plans for today?" asks Gunner, stepping closer to me.

"Why?"

"I'd like to make up for last night."

Thoughts of Gunner's face pressed between my legs flash through my mind. "How?" I ask.

"I'd like to take you and Evie out for the day."

"Yes, please, Mummy, please, can we?"

Gunner raises a cocky eyebrow because he knows he's already won.

A couple hours later, Gunner pulls the car into a large car park. I smile to myself as Evie squeals in delight at the flashing lights and music coming from the fun fair. She loves fairground rides, and I plan to make Gunner suffer by going on them all with her.

I move to get the pushchair from the back of the car, but Gunner stops me. "I'll carry her if she gets too tired."

"She gets heavy, Gunner. I'll get the pushchair."

He shakes his head, getting Evie from the car. "I don't like when kids are sat in the pushchair with crowds all around them. It must be scary, and she won't see anything."

I shrug. "Fine, whatever you say."

Secretly, I love that he's thinking about Evie like this, and I follow them into the entrance with a smile on my face.

"I want to go there," orders Evie, pointing to a child's train.

I inwardly laugh. This is my chance to embarrass Gunner. I'm about to tell him he needs to go on the ride with her, but before I have a chance, he looks inside the cart of the ride. "There's no safety belt in here, Princess, so I'll have to come on with you. Is that okay?" Evie nods enthusiastically, and I watch as he places her in the cart before sliding in beside her and placing his arm around her.

I laugh. "Oh my god, you look huge. I need to evidence this." I whip out my phone, and Gunner pulls Evie tighter to him, posing for the picture.

The rest of the day goes pretty much the same. Gunner squeezes himself into every child-friendly ride and refuses to let me pay for any of it, despite me constantly trying to hand him money or get in there first to pay. He buys us lunch from the burger cart followed by candy floss, insisting that no fun fair trip is complete without the sweet, fluffy treat. Evie eventually lets out a yawn and settles her head against Gunner's shoulder.

"Thanks for today. I've really enjoyed it, and so has Evie," I say. Despite us being surrounded by good men who love us dearly, we've never had a day out like this.

He smiles down at me, and I feel a familiar flutter in my stomach. "That's okay, I've loved today. You have a great little girl here."

I smile at Evie, who's gone to sleep in Gunner's strong arms. It's enough to melt any girl's heart. "I do," I agree.

We get back to the clubhouse and Gunner insists on carrying a sleeping Evie from the car. Inside, he wanders into the main room, ignoring his brothers by the bar and heading straight over to the sofas. He gently lays her down, pulling a blanket from the back of it and placing it over her.

"Wow, I think my ovaries just burst," whispers Gemma. I laugh, nudging her with my shoulder.

"He's been really great with her today. He even managed to bargain with her mid-tantrum."

"That is good." Gemma grins, knowing how Evie's terrible twos tantrums can cause World War three. "Hate to burst the family vibe, but Cammie arrived about ten minutes ago, said Gunner texted her to meet him here."

I try to keep the smile on my face, but I know it falters. "There's no family vibe. He was making up for a misunderstanding."

I watch Cammie join Gunner. He wraps her under his arm and holds her against his side, kissing her on the head. "Lucky bitch," mutters Gemma.

I sit myself at the bar and ask Tap for a bottle of water. Gunner and Cammie approach me. "Can Cammie join you while I go and get changed?" asks Gunner.

I nod and offer a fake smile, pointing to the stool next to me.

Once Gunner's gone, Cammie turns to me, a nervous smile playing on her lips. "Ava, I know you're protective of Ashton, but I just wanted to say that I really do like him and I don't plan on hurting him, if that's what you're worried about."

"I'm not protective. We haven't really seen each other properly for almost three years. In fact, he drives me insane."

She frowns. "I just get the impression you're not exactly thrilled about me being around."

I laugh to hide how mortified I am. "It makes no difference to me, Cammie. Women come and go from this club, and Gunner is no different from the other guys here. It's a waste of time getting to know any girls they bring back because they don't last." I hide my wince well. Gunner will kill me, and judging by the hurt on Cammie's face, he'll get to hear about this conversation. I don't know why I said it, it was a bitch move, and I feel bad instantly. "Look, I didn't mean it like that—" I start, but Gunner returns, cutting my sentence short.

"You ready?" he asks, kissing Cammie on the lips.

She nods but doesn't speak, and he pulls back, frowning. "What?" he asks. Cammie shakes her head but doesn't use words, which concerns him more. "Cammie, what?" She glances at me, and Gunner clicks on straight away. "What did you say?" he snaps, his eyes flashing with anger.

"It came out wrong," I say, biting my lower lip.

"What. Did. You. Say?" he asks, punctuating every word.

"Something about not bothering to get to know the girls that you guys bring back because they don't last." I cringe as I finish the sentence, waiting for his rage.

"Shit move, Ava. What a way to ruin the day we've just had. I like Cammie, and you need to accept it."

The fact he sounds disappointed in me hurts more than if he was to lose his shit and yell at me. I stand. "Sorry, Cammie, I didn't mean all the guys. I was just shooting my mouth off without thinking."

Gunner shakes his head. "Just because you fucked your life up, doesn't mean you can be bitter about mine."

I take a step back. "I didn't fuck it up. Evie is a blessing, not a damn curse."

"You chose a good-for-nothing dick to be her father, that's where you fucked up. She deserves a good man in her life, and you can't even tell us who he is because you're that embarrassed."

I let out a frustrated growl. "Why do you care so much? It's in the past. I'm sorry if I upset you, Cammie, I didn't mean to. Gunner cockblocked me last night, and so I thought I'd pay him back. I shouldn't have done that to you. It's not your fault he's a complete and utter prick."

"It wasn't cockblocking, Ava. Jackson is welcome to you anytime, just not in the bathroom I have to use."

Damien swings the door to his office open. "What's going on in here?"

"Your sister needs to grow the fuck up," yells Gunner.

He rolls his eyes. "Right, you two, get the fuck in here now," he mutters, pointing to his office. I stomp behind Gunner like a brat, and Damien slams the office door behind us both.

"This stops today. I can't have you both at each other's throats. I love you both and seeing you like this is tearing me up. What happened to make you turn against each other?" When we don't reply, he sighs. "Fine. This stops today. Talk." I watch in horror as he steps from the office, closing the door behind him. We hear the lock, and I rush over to it, pulling on the handle, "Damien, what the hell?"

"Sort it out. No one leaves the office until it's sorted," shouts Damien through the locked door.

"Don't be a prick, Damien, I have a date," shouts Gunner.

"And I have Evie to look after," I add.

"I'll take care of both, now, get talking."

I flop down in the chair, folding my arms in a sulky gesture. "Great."

"This is your fault. If you'd kept your mouth shut, we wouldn't have argued. We had a good day. Why'd you ruin it?"

I shrug. "I don't know," I mutter. "It came out wrong."

"It came out exactly as you meant it to. Ava, I don't know what your problem is, but I like Cammie and I don't want you ruining it because of your stupid little crush."

I feel my face heat up as anger rushes through my veins. "Stupid little crush?" I repeat. "That was years ago, Gunner, and that's all it was, a damn crush. I've moved on. I have a child with someone else and a life. You are not and never will be part of that." My heart races in my chest, and I hate how he turns on me. One minute, we're sharing my daughter at the fun fair and enjoying her delight together, and then he's pulling me up about a crush I had when I was a teenager.

"Then don't try and put Cammie off me," he snaps.

"I was being honest about the guys around here. I didn't mean you exactly, but it came out wrong. It isn't what I meant. She needs to stop being so sensitive if she's going to be an old lady."

"I love her just the way she is, thanks. I don't want no hard-faced bitch who doesn't give a shit."

I note that he uses the word 'love' and it sends a dagger straight to my heart. "Then she won't last two minutes. The club girls will have her running to you in tears at every opportunity. They smell fear," I warn.

"Let me worry about that. You just concentrate on looking after your fatherless kid and stay the fuck out of my life. I tried to make things right between us today, and this is how you repay me."

"Jesus, Gunner, you always go for the throat. Does Cammie cry every time you argue, or do you save the cutting comments especially for me?" I snap. "It really grates your shit that my child doesn't have a father around, and I'm not sure why because it's nothing to do with you. And I never asked for today. You don't have to make things right between us, just stay out of my way."

Gunner sits in Damien's chair behind the desk, heaving his large black boots onto the polished wood and leaning back. The chair creaks under his large frame. "You heard Damien. We're the closest people to him, and he wants us to get along. We were friends once."

"That was before you treated me like club arse and then humiliated me," I mutter, fiddling with the hem of my T-shirt. "If D knew about that, he'd think differently."

"So, that's the real issue then, how we left it before?"

I stand abruptly and head for the door. "I'm not doing this. I'm a grown woman and I've moved on."

Gunner jumps up, following me. He catches my wrist and turns me to face him. "I was an arse back then. I thought I was doing it for the best."

I take a shuddery breath. "You treated me like the most important thing in your world that night, and then you woke up and looked at me like I was a stranger. You acted like I'd stalked you and you'd done me this great act of kindness by sleeping with me." Tears threaten to fall, and I bite the inside of my cheek, something I do when I'm stressed.

He looks guilty. "I didn't want you to follow me. I wanted you to go to Uni and live your life. I knew you liked me and—"

"And you thought you were that amazing, that I'd give up my dreams and run around the world after you?" I laugh and pull my wrist from his grip. "I would have happily walked away after that night and not given you a second thought."

"You gave up your dreams and got fucking pregnant," he yells.

I growl in frustration. It always comes back to this. "I don't know how to explain it to you any clearer than I already have. I love my daughter and I don't regret a second of her. I still followed my dreams and, yes, I chose not to be with the father because he was a one-night stand. I had a lot of them after you. I chose to keep my baby and bring her up here with my family. You are the only one who seems to think I gave up my dreams when, in actual fact, I made a better life for myself."

"You're not that type of girl. One-night stands are not you," he growls.

"How would you know? You don't know me anymore, Gunner," I say, exasperation in my voice. "I am not the same little girl who followed you around. I grew up, and thanks to you, I saw what men are really like. Men are meant to care and say all the right things, until they get what they want and then they treat you like shit. So, now, I don't give them the opportunity. I take what I want and move on." A stray tear rolls down my cheek and I brush it away quickly, folding my arms across my chest.

"Ava, I'm so sorry," he whispers, placing a hand on my shoulder. I shrug it off as the weight of my confession hangs between us, and I feel more humiliated now than I ever did. Is that why I do what I do, to keep men away? I've never really thought too much about it until now, but I guess I do blame Gunner. I trusted him, and he broke my heart.

"Damien, open the door!" I bang on it hard with my fist.

"Ava, we need to sort this out." Gunner sighs, standing behind me. The heat of his body wraps around me, and I resist the urge to turn around and bury my face in his hard chest.

"It's too late, Gunner. We need to accept that we have nothing left to save between us and go on with our lives. It's okay to not like each other. There's no law that says we have to be best friends just because of Damien."

Gunner places his hand back to my shoulder and gently turns me to face him. "I thought I was saving you from me. Turns out, I didn't save you at all." If only he knew just how true that statement was.

I hear Damien's footsteps approach the door. "Have you two kissed and made up?" he shouts.

I go to reply, but Gunner slaps a large hand over my mouth, pulling me back against him and away from the door. "Not yet, Pres. I'll give you a call when we're done."

"No problem, Gunner. Cammie is fine. She's eating pizza with some of the ol' ladies, getting to know them."

Once we hear Damien's footsteps move away, Gunner uncovers my mouth. "We aren't leaving until we've talked this over."

He pushes me to sit on the small couch, then he goes to the drinks cabinet and pulls out a bottle of whisky, grabbing two glasses. He sits next to me, his enormous frame taking up most of the room. I shuffle up as best I can, trying to move my thigh away from his. I take the glass he offers, and he fills it with the amber liquid.

"Right, let's talk," he says firmly.

"Cammie's waiting."

"This is important. Besides, it'll do her good to get to know some of the girls."

"Are you claiming her, Gunner?" The question comes out quiet, and I take a gulp of the whisky, coughing when it burns my throat.

He shrugs. "I really like her, and she's the first one I've liked since . . ." He trails off, knocking his own drink back. "Loads of one-night stands?" he asks, changing the subject.

I offer a sad smile. "I'm not proud, I went a bit crazy for a while."

"Because of me?"

I shake my head, biting on my lower lip. "Not just you."

"Because of Evie's dad, or because of what happened years ago?"

I take a deep breath and let it out slowly, "He isn't a good man, Gunner. I don't talk about him because he isn't worth it. If Damien went digging about, it might bring him back, and then he would know I have Evie. He would use her to get to the club."

"I don't know anyone stupid enough to mess with this club, Ava."

"As for the other thing, leave it in the past. I have," I say.

I look down and my glass is empty. Gunner refills it, and I take a few big swallows, loving the way the buzz relaxes me.

"So, are you gonna announce that you've claimed Cammie?"

"I haven't claimed her, not yet. She gets me, yah know. She doesn't expect anything, and she gets me. I can be myself around her. It reminds me of how things were with us before I fucked it all up."

Gunner's right, things were good for us before we spent that night together. There was always the right amount of flirting to get the butterflies fluttering in my stomach, but we also laughed together and hung out. I enjoyed being around him. It burns me to know he feels that way about Cammie, but if he feels so strongly about her, then I have to accept her.

"I felt the same about you back then. I liked that you were crushing on me because I liked you too, but it was just never the right time. I didn't want to upset Pops, and then I thought it would piss Damien off, and I didn't want to ruin our friendship. When you told me you got into Uni, it crushed me, but I wanted you to be free to follow that dream. Every time you came back in the first year, I wanted to drag you off and keep you with me. When I knew I was going in the Army, I knew I wouldn't see you as much." He pauses and sighs. "It was a shit thing to do, but that last night before I left, I lost control. After years of denying myself, I couldn't stop it."

I nod, taking the bottle from him and topping up my glass. "I wasn't exactly fighting you off." I'm reeling from his confession—he liked me back, and I never knew.

"I shouldn't have gone there." He shrugs. "If I'd known I was the first since..." He trails off. At the time, I didn't want to break the spell. He'd ripped at my clothes with such passion and desperation that I was scared to stop him for fear that he'd realise he didn't really want me.

"Does Cammie know we have history?"

He shakes his head. "No, and I'd prefer it to stay that way. I'd like you to get along, and it might make it hard for her if she knew."

I refrain from telling him how hard it will be for me. "Secrets already. You better tell the club girls not to spread rumours about you getting blowjobs out back then."

He groans, placing his glass on the floor and swigging from the bottle direct. "Remember that time we nearly kissed? I think I was fifteen, so you were, what, eleven?" He smiles.

I nod. Of course, I remember that day. I thought I was going to die from the way my heart beat out my chest. "Yeah, I remember."

"But my half-brother turned up, interrupting us. I hated that bastard, and that just made me hate him more." He laughs.

The thought of Gunner's brother sends a chill down my spine. Michael is older than Gunner by two years. He was only one when his dad, Tank, left his mum and hooked up with Gunner's mum. Tank was the VP to my pops and was known for his love of club girls. Gunner's mum worked the bar, and after a stormy fling, Tank became obsessed with her. They fell in love, and she got pregnant with Gunner. Tank soon left his first wife and son. His actions sent Michael's mum on a downward spiral, and she became depressed and hooked on all kinds of drugs. She died when Michael was in his twenties, but Gunner hadn't had anything to do with him since way before then. Michael blamed their dad for the poor choices that his mum made and refused to have anything to do with Gunner or Gunner's mum.

"Are you okay?" Gunner interrupts my thoughts. I take the bottle from him and drink some more.

"How is Michael? Have you heard from him?"

He snorts, disgust on his face. "Nah, he moved away about three or four years ago."

After a short pause, he turns sideways, his thigh pressing against mine. "So, you and Jackson? I didn't see that one coming."

"He likes me," I shrug, "and he's a good-looking guy."

"He can't keep his dick in his pants."

I laugh. "I don't want anything serious. Jackson turns up every few weeks, and I'm happy with that."

"And if he wanted to claim you?"

I laugh again. "He won't ever claim anyone, and like I said, I don't want anything serious. I have Evie to think about."

"Do you wonder what would have happened if we had admitted how we felt?"

I shake my head. "We weren't meant to be, and I wouldn't have Evie if we'd gotten together."

"Damn right, cos I'd have killed anyone who looked at you. But maybe we'd have our own kid now."

CHAPTER SIX

Gunner

Ava avoids looking at me, chewing on that damn lip, looking sexy as hell. I drink down some more whisky. I need to get back to Cammie before I fuck this up. Ava stretches out, her arms going over her head, and I watch her shirt pull tight across her breasts.

"I really don't want to think how you'd be with a kid, Gunner. You'd have a guy following Evie round nursery if she were yours."

I laugh, but she's right—I'd be a protective motherfucker. "Evie doesn't have to be mine for me to go bat shit crazy over her welfare. You remember how D and I were over you?"

She rolls her eyes. "Don't remind me. The first guy I kissed pissed himself when you and Damien turned up mid-kiss."

"That's cos he was a pussy."

"Gunner, he was ten years old," Ava says with a laugh.

I grin, remembering his geeky glasses and mouth full of braces. He'd taken Ava to the school disco and then thought he'd get a cheeky kiss in. "I just wanted to be him, the little fucker," I confess with a cocky smile.

Ava shifts uncomfortably. "You'd better get back to Cammie. Someone else might claim her if you leave her too long."

"I'd like to see them try," I growl, and I see that little flash of hurt in her eyes that she hides so well. "I already lost out on a chance with you, I can't miss out again."

"Please, you never had a chance with me," she says with a grin. "I had them lining up to claim me."

I tug her ponytail, forcing her head to face me. "I made sure D kept them all away."

"So, you're the reason I'm still on the shelf at twenty-four?"

I stare into her stormy blue eyes, her teeth chewing on her lip, and I feel like she's daring me to kiss her, to make that move. We don't speak as I wrap her hair tighter in my fist, warring with myself. And then I move forward, pressing my lips hard against hers. Her hand comes up and grips my shoulder, giving her enough hold to haul herself up and onto my lap.

We kiss hungrily, and she rubs herself against me shamelessly as I run my hands across the soft skin covering her ribs. I slowly move them up and across her front, her breasts filling the palms of my hands perfectly. She groans when I run my thumbs across the peaks of her nipples straining through the lace of her bra.

She tugs at my T-shirt, and I grip the hem, pulling it up over my head. Ava runs her hands over my hard chest, her eyes tracing over the tattoos that cover my skin.

"Stand," I order. She looks at me warily but rises to her feet without question. "Get them off," I say, pointing to her leggings. Without hesitation, she pushes them down her legs and then proceeds to remove her top. I stand before it's even hit the floor and sweep her into my arms. She wraps her legs around my waist, and I thrust my tongue into her mouth, swiping at hers hungrily.

Her hands wrap around my neck, and she holds on while I unfasten my jeans, pushing them down enough to release my hard cock. I reach into my back pocket, pulling out my wallet, and fumble around until I have a condom.

Ava kisses down my neck and across my shoulder, nipping and biting. Once the condom is in place, I press her hard against the wall, pulling at her bra until her breasts are spilling out over the lace. I gently run my tongue over a soft pink peak, and she shivers.

I know I should stop, and somewhere in the back of my mind, there's a voice screaming at me not to put my dick in her again. I remember the feeling of her milking my cock and the way her face flushes before she comes, and suddenly, the need to have that again outweighs any rational thoughts. I grip my cock in my hand, lining it up with her opening. Ava stares into my eyes, panting, waiting to see if I'll go through with it.

I slowly push into her, our eyes locked onto one another, as I stretch her inch by inch. She's biting her lip so hard, I'm surprised it isn't bleeding. "You want me to stop?" I whisper, and she shakes her head, panic in her eyes, "You want my cock?"

"Yes," she groans, throwing her head back as I push the final few inches in hard. Once I'm all the way in, I still, letting her adjust. Her fingernails are digging into my shoulders, and I know there'll be marks there, but I'm too far gone to care.

After a few seconds, she begins to wriggle, trying to get me to move. I take her nipple into my mouth, and she lets out little gasps.

"Hold on," I pant, and she wraps her legs tighter around my hips.

I begin to move, slow at first, and then I lose control, ramming into her at a fast pace. She begins to cry out, and I place my hand over her mouth, muffling her cries. I feel her stiffen, so I slow down, halting her orgasm. "Gunner," she moans in frustration.

I grin, wanting her to beg me. "What do you want, Bait?"

"You know what I want," she whines as I pick the pace back up.

I build her up and slow down again, and she hits against my chest with her fist. "We don't have time to fuck about." She's right.

"Say my name," I pant.

"Gunner," she replies smartly, and I ram into her hard, "Okay, Ash. Ashton. Fuck."

I feel her shudder and then she buries her face against my shoulder as an orgasm rips through her. I keep my eyes on the flush of her cheeks and the curve of her mouth as I build up to my own release, pulling her head back by her hair so I can watch her as I fuck her hard. I follow her orgasm, clamping my jaw shut tight so I don't yell out. I think it's the hardest I've come in years, and I feel dizzy and lightheaded as all the blood rushes to my cock.

I walk us over to the couch, still joined together, not ready to lose her yet. I sit down, and she rests her head on my shoulder. I'm still semi-hard, which isn't unusual for me, and if I move, I'll get hard again and could end up fucking her over and over. As tempting as that sounds, right now, I know I have to go back out there and face Cammie.

Guilt begins to creep its way into my chest, and I shut my eyes tight, resting my head on the back of the couch while I draw lazy circles along Ava's back. She sits up slightly and places her hands behind her, resting them on my knees. Her breasts jut forward, and I open one eye. Ava gently rocks forward, my cock jumping to life again.

"Age hasn't changed you then." She smirks, moving back and forth slowly.

I eye her, not moving or commenting as she grips her breasts and gently squeezes her nipples. I watch her take her pleasure, moving at her own pace and using her expert fingers to get another release. I lock my fingers around the back of my head, not daring to touch her because I know I'll want more and I'm already thinking up excuses for Cammie.

I growl in frustration, resting my head on the back of the couch and throwing an arm over my eyes. Ava stills, her deep breaths the only sound in the room. "You're regretting it," she mutters. It's more of a statement than a question.

I let out a long, slow breath and then lift my head up to look at her. Her beautiful face is flushed pink and her lips are swollen from our eager kisses. "It's not regret . . . maybe guilt," I say slowly.

She gives a slight nod and then lifts herself from me. I watch her carefully as she picks up her discarded clothes and starts to dress. "Ava, listen—"

"If you even dare utter the word 'sorry', I'll punch you in the face," she mutters.

I press my lips together. "I am sorry. Not sorry that it happened but . . ." I trail off. I don't even know what I'm sorry for. Being with her feels right, but the timing is so wrong, again. All I can think about is Cammie and how hurt she'll be, and then Damien and how he will react. Fuck, this is so messed up.

Ava goes over to the door and bangs hard. "Damien, open this damn door!" Seconds later, we hear his heavy footfalls and then the key clicking in the lock.

"Took your goddamn time," Damien grumbles as the door swings open. He looks up and stares at Ava's face for a second and then mine. "You okay, Ava? You look upset."

She shrugs and moves past him. "We'll try harder to be civil to each other," she says as she passes.

He nods, eyeing me suspiciously. "That's all I can ask. Pops is in the bar wondering where you are. Go and have a drink with the old bastard."

Ava leaves, and Damien shuts the door. "What happened?"

"She just told you, we agreed to be civil," I say, shifting uncomfortably on the couch.

"You both have that 'just fucked' look." His face is seriously pissed-off, and I stand just in case I have to fight my way out of here.

"Don't be ridiculous, Damien. Ava hates me, and I have a girl." I head for the door. "You coming for that drink? I have an announcement to make."

Damien follows me out to the bar, where Ava sits on a stool chatting to her father. Cammie makes a beeline for me, smiling. She tucks herself into my side and the guilt twists in my stomach. Damien is still watching me closely. The guy isn't stupid, he suspects.

Damien bangs his hand on the bar a few times to get everyone's attention. There aren't too many guys around, so it quiets down pretty quick. "Gunner has an announcement to make," he shouts.

I feel Ava's eyes on me, but I refuse to make contact as I cough to clear my throat. I feel like the guilt is choking me.

"Finally admitting your undying love for me, Gunner?" Pops pipes up with a laugh.

I roll my eyes. "You're way too old for me, Grandpa." I grip Cammie's hand and hold her to me. "I just wanted to let you guys know that I'm finally taking an ol' lady, I hope Cammie fits in well with our family, and I hope you all love her as much as I do."

The announcement is met with cheers and jests about fidelity. I risk a glance to the bar where Ava sits as stiff as stone, staring at me with shock in her expression.

It's a dick move, but what else am I supposed to do? Ava has a kid with someone else. Her brother is my President, and he'd see it as disrespect to him if we got together. And her Pops treats me like his own. She and I can never work, so the only logical thing to do is claim Cammie. I like Cammie a lot, she gets me, and I guess this was always going to be my end game, but circumstances have brought this day sooner than expected.

We're hugged by the other ol' ladies, and I'm slapped on the back by the guys. Damien kisses Cammie on the cheek and says, "Welcome to the family, Cameron."

Ava appears next to Damien and smiles awkwardly. She hugs Cammie and then turns to me.

"Congratulations." She hugs me and kisses me lightly on the cheek. I close my eyes, breathing in her vanilla scent. Pain stabs at my heart, but I know this is for the best.

"I'm so sorry," I whisper into her ear.

Ava pulls away abruptly when Evie bounds in and wraps her arms around Ava's leg. "I made biscuits with Grandma."

Ava picks her up. "Wow, I hope you saved me one."

Evie reaches her arms out to me, and I take her, happy that she wants to come to me. "I made Gunner one."

"Let's go eat biscuits, shorty," I say, heading for the kitchen, glad to be away from Ava's frostiness.

Damien barges into the kitchen five minutes later and grabs a biscuit off the cooling rack. "I'm calling church, something's come up."

The guys are already in the room by the time I get in there. Taking my seat, I notice Pops has joined us. "What's going on, Damien?" I ask.

He waits for everyone to quiet down. "So, Pops has some news on the new chief of police. After a bit of digging, because they were all a little hush hush about it, he got a name." Damien pauses, glancing at me. "It's Michael . . . Michael Gunn."

I frown at the sound of my brother's name. "Hey?"

Damien nods. "As in your brother, Gunner."

I sit quietly, letting my brain process this new information. "He ain't my brother, D."

"Half-brother. Either way, the fucker is in at the top. This obviously poses a problem for us seeing as he hates The Eagles," says Pops. "He never forgave your father for leaving him and his mum, and I wouldn't put it past the bastard to have joined just to fuck us over."

I run my hands over my tired face. This day is going from bad to worse. Ava hates me, I've cheated on my girl, and now, my shithead half-brother is the chief. This fucks the club over because there's no way he'll make any deals with us.

"So, now what?" asks Grill. "I've got a lorry load of class A coming in the next week or so. There's no way I'll get it through customs if he finds out. He'll have every port, train, and airport checked for any shipments to us."

"I've invited him for a chat. We're having a get-together for the local community this Saturday. It'll be a push to pull it off at this short notice, but I couldn't think of another reason to get him to meet us. It'll be a chance for him to get to know the locals and for us to look like we're above board now. Make sure everything is completely legit, no drugs, no whores, and no fighting. I want him to leave here with the impression that we've turned this club around. Grill, put a hold on the shipment for now. We can afford to delay it for another couple of weeks."

Grill nods in agreement, pulling out his phone and making the call.

"Do you want me around on Saturday, Pres, or should I lie low?" I ask.

Damien contemplates my question, glancing at Pops for direction. Pops nods before adding, "Be around. Make sure you and Cammie are the picture of love. Maybe he's grown up a bit in the last few years."

We can all hope, I think to myself.

CHAPTER SEVEN

Ava

Gemma sits back in her seat and stares at me open-mouthed. "But he just announced he's claiming Cammie."

I'd texted her and Chloe an SOS message, and they arrived pretty much straight away. We sit in the bar of the club, which has gone quiet since the guys went into church.

"Yes, I know, Gemma, that's my point. He's a twat and I hate him."

Chloe drinks her vodka back in one gulp and winces. "You fell for it again?"

I glare at her. "Thanks, Chlo, really helpful."

Chloe shrugs. "But you did. Why would you go there again after what happened before? And when his girl is waiting in the next room," she whisper-hisses. She pauses and then smiles. "Actually, that is completely hot. It's something I'd totally do."

"Look, I could do without Judgy MacJudgy, thanks. My hangover is setting in, and I hate myself right now. Give me support and tell me I'll feel better in the morning. Be good girlfriends," I huff. They exchange a look that says I'm asking too much of them, and I roll my eyes.

"Look, we love you, Ava, but seriously, you pined after this guy for years, and the minute you're alone together, you jump his bones," says Gemma. "Even though he totally shattered your heart three years ago, and he told you he really liked Cammie five minutes before you fucked him. What were you thinking?"

"Whisky had a huge part to play in all this," I cry. "Aargh, I'm so stupid."

"Tell me you used a condom, because if you get pregnant again, I think your brother may actually have a mental breakdown," says Gemma. "Is he going to tell Cammie?"

"I hope not. He didn't even tell her we had a thing years back, so I doubt it."

The guys must have finished church because the bar suddenly fills up. Damien approaches, his eyes fixed on Chloe, who stares at me, purposefully not making eye contact with him.

"Ladies, how are you all fixed for Saturday? Let's dust off the barbeque and have an open day for the locals."

When we don't reply, he sighs. "Look, I have the new chief of police coming, so it's a big deal. I'd like the whole family to show. I want to give off the family vibe."

Chloe smiles. "I have a date on Saturday night, but I'll come for a few hours in the afternoon."

"With who?" he asks, fire igniting in his eyes.

"You wouldn't know him. We met through work."

"You not wanting your bed to get cold?" snaps Damien, and Chloe scowls at him.

"It's been three months since Darren left. I'm pretty sure in that time you've slept with a different woman every night," she huffs.

Chloe is probably right. My brother has a string of women ready to keep him warm whenever he clicks his fingers, and he's never had a serious girlfriend or anyone who's come close. Taking on the club young was his priority, and with the title came free and willing pussy. What young guy would turn that down?

Chloe is so in love with Damien. When she met Darren, I thought she'd moved on, but even during her year together with him, she still flirted with my brother. If he had told her to dump Darren, I have no doubt she would have. The trouble is, Damien doesn't want to settle down. I think he's scared to claim someone in case it makes them a target. He talks about getting the club straight first, but who knows how long that will take.

"Are you keeping an eye on who I'm fucking, Chloe? A bit stalker-like, don't you think?"

"Why don't you invite your date to the barbeque?" I suggest, trying to break up the nasty vibes flying back and forth.

"No, that's not a good idea," snaps Damien, glaring at me.

Chloe smiles. "Yeah, great thinking. I'll text him now."

Chloe pulls out her phone, and I grin at Damien's annoyed expression. It's payback for locking me in that room today with Gunner.

By the time Saturday rolls around, I'm exhausted. I worked daytime shifts on Thursday and Friday, and Evie didn't sleep too well on Thursday night. The last thing I feel like doing is spending the day and evening chatting with the locals and being friendly, trying to prove we're good people and worth being part of their community. But that's exactly what I have to do.

Damien's rented bouncy castles and other inflatables to entertain the kids, and there's a DJ and an outdoor bar. The place is packed out, and poor Grill looks exhausted with all the cooking, as does Tap as he tends the bar.

I stand with a small glass of wine, watching Evie from a distance while she throws her tiny frame around on the bouncy castle. She loves days like this because all the other club kids come and she gets to run around crazy. I smile at the memories that flood my mind from when I was a kid doing the exact same thing.

Suddenly, someone approaches me from behind. "Well, fancy seeing you here."

My breath catches in my throat and every part of my body tenses at the deep voice as he presses his mouth to the side of my head. I turn slowly, praying it isn't him, but my hope dies at the sight of his smarmy smile and hateful eyes.

"Michael." My voice comes out tight and croaky.

"You look amazing, Ava. Curves in all the right places." He assesses me, his eyes roaming up and down my body. I fold my arms over my chest, trying to stop my hand from shaking and spilling my wine.

"What are you doing here? I didn't know you were back in town."

"Damien invited me."

As if conjured, Damien appears. "You made it. Good to see you, Michael." They shake hands. "You remember Ava?"

Michael nods, a smirk on his lips, "How could I forget the club princess."

"I have to go and . . ." I trail off. "Excuse me."

Making a dash to the toilets inside the clubhouse, I chuck my wine into the sink, not paying attention as it splashes over the countertop. I dive into the nearest stall and hunch over the toilet basin, dry heaving. Lowering to my knees, I brace my hands on either side of the stall. My eyes water and the coughing stings my dry throat. After a couple minutes, I stand, trying to pull myself together. *I'm safe, and the guys are all here.* I repeat those words in my head as I rinse my face, the cold water cooling the heat of my clammy skin. I can't stay in here all day, so I take a few deep breaths. I need to find Chloe or Gemma.

I open the door and crash straight into a hard body. Instantly, I know it's Michael because of the distinct scent of his aftershave. It's all citrus and bitter, and I hate it. He steadies me with his hands, which feel cold on my damp skin. "Steady, gorgeous," he says, smiling down at me. The way his dark eyes assess me creeps me out. It's like I can see every disgusting thought in his head written all over his cruel face. "Does Gunner know you're here?" I ask.

His face changes from smarmy to hate. "I haven't seen him yet. I'm more interested in catching up with you."

Michael runs a finger down my arm, and I shudder. He must mistake this for pleasure because he takes my wrist and pulls me gently towards him. "Michael, I have to get back out there," I stutter.

"Don't deny me, baby. It's been so long." He leans down like he's going to kiss me, and I blink a few times, trying to stop any sign of tears.

The main door crashes against the wall and little footsteps run towards me. "Mummy, guess what," screeches Evie. She throws herself at me, and I automatically catch her, stepping back from Michael, who eyes Evie with interest.

"Sweetie, please go and find Uncle Dam. I'll be out in a minute." As if sensing my unease, she grips me tighter and stares at Michael from behind her hair.

"You have a kid?" he asks, frowning.

"Yes," I nod, "she's three." And then I close my eyes because I instantly know Evie will correct me. Without hesitation, she huffs in that little madam way she pulls off so well.

"No, Mummy, two."

I place her on the floor. "Go to Uncle Damien, now." Evie looks hurt by my brisk tone, but she runs back outside.

"Are you fucking serious right now?" growls Michael.

"It's not what you think," I begin, but his hand dashes out, grabbing my arm and dragging me back into the bathroom.

He locks the door and turns on me. "Get talking."

"I had a one-night stand. I didn't know the guy and I fell pregnant. It was just after you left."

"I don't fucking believe you, Ava. I can see it in her eyes, she's mine."

I shake my head, tears springing to my eyes. "No, Michael, she isn't yours."

"It's written all over your pretty little face. If she isn't mine, you won't mind doing a DNA test."

I swipe at the tears. "I'm telling the truth."

He moves in close, pressing me against the sink. I turn my head away, but he pulls me back to face him. "You always were terrible at lying. You're bringing my daughter up in this shithole with these criminals? You make me sick. I want that DNA test, and then we need to talk about how you're going to make things right."

"Please, Michael, don't cause problems. I don't want anything from you. Go back to wherever you went to before. I won't come after you for money." I begin to cry, hating myself for being so vulnerable in front of him. He gets off on this, and I see the delight in his eyes.

"I'm not going anywhere, gorgeous. This is my town now. I'm the new chief of police."

I close my eyes, soaking up the realisation that Michael is here to stay and he will fuck this club up. That's the reason he's back.

He grips my chin in his fingers roughly, forcing me to look at him. His cold eyes dance with desire, and I battle hard to hold myself together. He leans closer, smiling at my obvious disgust. "I fucking missed these lips."

He presses a kiss to the side of my mouth, and I let out a squeak in protest, which only spurs him on. He licks along my bottom lip and then his mouth is on mine, hungrily pushing his tongue into my mouth. His hands run up my ribs and then around to my breasts, where he squeezes hard, and he presses his noticeable erection against my stomach.

"Maybe we can come to an arrangement like before," he whispers, smiling against my lips. "Give me your phone." I reach into my back pocket and hand my phone to him. There's no point in denying him—I've learnt that the hard way. He adds his number and then rings his phone so he has mine. "I'll call you, and you'd better come. If you don't, I'll make all kinds of trouble, gorgeous."

"It's not easy for me to just up and come. I work shifts, I have Evie, and Damien doesn't let me anywhere without someone tailing me."

"Then you'll have to convince him. Tell him about you and me," he suggests with a wink, "about our history."

"I'm serious, it's not like before."

He suddenly grips my throat. "I don't want excuses, Ava. I'm going to sort a DNA test out, and you will bring that kid when I text you. You do that test, then we come to an arrangement. Understand?"

I nod, and he smiles, releasing my throat.

"These are bigger," he says, lifting my top and ogling my breasts. I don't stop him because he'll just get nasty, and I don't want to alert any of the guys by walking out of here upset. Michael wants to cause trouble, especially for Damien and Gunner. Now that Michael is high up in the police force, we don't stand a chance against him.

I grip the sink, digging my nails into the hard marble. He rubs at my breasts, pulling down my bra, then he leans in and licks a nipple, making me cringe. He sucks it into his mouth and hums in delight.

"I can't wait. Let's get something started. How about you let me fuck your mouth, and I don't go and tell your brother that I'm part of your family now. I bet you didn't tell him our little secret, did you?"

When I don't answer, he grins. He has me exactly where he wants me. Unbuckling his trousers and releasing himself, he strokes his shaft with one hand and touches my breasts with the other. "Knees," he grits out.

I drop to my knees, humiliation spreading through me. He presses his tip against my lips, and I part them. He doesn't give me a chance to take him myself. Instead, he grips my hair and pushes straight into my mouth, making me gag.

He groans and pushes farther, his cock brushing against the back of my throat. I cough and choke, but this only encourages him to pull out and ram back in over and over.

He fucks my mouth, delighting in the fact that I'm struggling to breath. There's saliva dripping from my mouth, and he wipes it over my chest, moaning and pushing harder. Suddenly, he stills, and I feel his release hit the back of my throat. He shouts out, pushing one last time and holding it halfway down my throat causing me to choke. I try to pull away, but he doesn't let me, and I hit at his legs, trying to get him to release me. When I finally get free, I fall on to all fours, gasping for breath and coughing, his taste lingering on my tongue.

"I missed you, Ava. I'll be in touch," he promises, tucking himself back inside his trousers.

I stay on the floor until I hear the door close behind him, and then I scrabble to my feet and lock the door, so he can't come back. I burst into tears, my body shuddering from my sobs. I catch a glimpse of myself in the mirror. My mascara is smudged down my face and my throat is red from where he gripped it. I'm suddenly transported back to years before, seeing myself as that same vulnerable girl, and I hate myself for it.

I spend some time cleaning my face, trying to make sure I look less harassed, and then I leave the bathroom to find Evie. She isn't used to me being so sharp-tongued with her, and I need to make sure she's okay. I find her in Gunner's arms, chatting to Brick, but when he catches sight of me, he stops mid-conversation.

"Are you okay, Bait?"

"Stop fucking calling me Bait. Give her to me," I snap, reaching for Evie.

Gunner frowns and then a look of irritation passes over his face. "I know you're pissed with me, but let's try and be civil," he growls, keeping hold of Evie.

"I want my daughter."

"I told her I'd take her on the bouncy castle."

"Gunner, give her to me." Tears fill my eyes. I know I'm overreacting and Gunner is looking at me like I've lost my mind, but I need to hold Evie and keep her away from Michael. "Do you know Michael's here?" I ask.

Gunner nods. "I knew he'd be coming. He's the chief of police apparently."

"Why didn't anyone tell me?" I wipe angrily at the tears as they leak down my cheeks.

"Ava, what are you so upset about? I'm fine. Michael doesn't worry me."

Trust Gunner to think this is all about him. I reach for Evie, and this time, he lets me take her from him. She protests and begins to cry, reaching back for him.

"Wondered when I'd see you, little brother." Michael's voice makes me want to vomit. I hold Evie close to me as she sobs.

Michael grins. "Oh dear, pretty little one, did Gunner make you cry?" he asks Evie.

"Michael, congratulations on the new job. Didn't even realise you'd joined the police force," says Gunner coldly.

Michael smiles wider, stuffing his hands in his pockets. "I'm surprised Ava didn't mention that. She saw me a few times when I was training."

All eyes turn to me as I shuffle uncomfortably. "I didn't think you'd want to know," I offer feebly. Gunner watches me closely, and I can see he's pissed I didn't mention it. I withheld important information from the club, which is not something I'd normally do. I can see questions whizzing around his head, but he won't ask them in front of Michael and highlight the lack of communication or trust.

"This kid yours and Ava's?" Michael asks. "Always knew you had a thing for each other."

"Why are you back here, Michael?" Gunner sighs, ignoring his question, and I find myself wondering why he hasn't corrected Michael.

"It's where I'm needed, Ashton. Apparently, the crime rate and drug running is ridiculously high here."

"The club keeps that shit straight. There ain't no drug problem around here."

"But you aren't the police, I am. Things will be done my way from now on." The pleasure on his face is sickening, and Gunner looks like he wants to smash his fist into it. "You two married or what?" he asks.

"We aren't together. Gunner has an ol' lady," I say bitterly, and Michael raises an eyebrow.

"You turned this away?" Michael grins, pointing at me. "She was practically your shadow and you turned her away for someone else? I don't know whether to high-five you or feel sorry for you, man."

"There was never anything between me and Ava," snaps Gunner.

"Well, if you're free and single, Ava, maybe I can take you out on a—"

Gunner is so quick, it takes me by surprise. He grips Michael's collar. "You stay the fuck away from Ava," he growls.

Michael's smug smile turns to me. "What do you say, Ava? Shall I give you a call?" His eyes are telling me what he wants to hear, and I'm scared that if I don't conform, he's going to bring my world down.

"Maybe, if you want to," I mumble with a shrug.

Gunner releases him with a shove and turns to me. "You'd better be fucking joking, Ava."

I avoid his steely glare and fix my eyes on Michael, who is now smirking, "I think I still have your number," he says. I watch with horror as he pulls out his mobile and scrolls through the screen. I feel the vibration of my mobile and then hear the shrill ringtone of Ed Sheeran's 'The A Team'.

"He's got your goddamn number!" yells Gunner. Evie jumps and clings to me tighter.

"What the fuck is going on over here?" hisses Damien as he approaches.

"Uncle Dam," shrieks Evie, reaching for him.

Damien takes her, glaring between me and Gunner. "I told you two to sort your shit out. Get out of my sight."

"With me, now," growls Gunner, grabbing my wrist and hauling me inside. He turns on me straight away. "Start talking, Ava."

Folding my arms, I look down at my feet. What can I say to him? Suddenly, everything I'd ever done to protect this club seems pointless. "I don't have to explain myself to you."

Gunner's face goes a deep shade of red, and I take a step back, scared that he'll explode.

"Let's get Damien in here, shall we, so you can explain why you kept it from the club that Michael was a cop . . . or why the fuck he has your number."

The door opens and Cammie comes in. Her smile fades when she sees us together. "Everything okay?" she asks, looking me up and down.

"No. Club business, Cam, wait outside." Gunner's brisk tone gets a glare from Cammie, and she folds her arms, stubbornness crossing her features.

"Club business with a woman? Thought that wasn't a thing," she snaps. Cammie's right—club business is for the guys and it isn't often the women of the club know any details about what goes down.

"Ava's different. She's club blood," lies Gunner.

"Or she's crushing on you, and you love it," huffs Cammie. I suddenly feel like I shouldn't be here, so I go to leave, but Gunner grabs my hand and then suddenly drops it when Cammie glares at the connection.

"Don't you dare go. We need to talk about this," he says to me and then turns to Cammie. "Baby, I can't talk about this with you right now. I will, but right now. I have to sort this," he says with a softness to his tone that he must only ever use with her.

Defiance is still firm on her face, and she looks at me. "Have you fucked him? Like ever?" I wasn't expecting the question, and my mouth opens and closes like a goldfish. I turn to look at Gunner, whose eyes are wide and staring back at me, probably wondering why lies don't roll off my tongue as easy as they do his.

Cammie slams a hand over her mouth. "Oh my god, you have. You told me . . . you swore there was nothing like that. You said she was a spoilt brat, the dumbass club princess who crushed on you but you didn't look at her like that!"

It's my turn to look and feel offended, and suddenly, Gunner doesn't look so sure of himself. The thought of him even saying those things hurts my heart, but to say them to her and then sleep with me for a second time kills me inside.

"You make me sick," I rage. "How dare you say that about me when you know how I feel about being labelled like that? I didn't ask to be treated like the fucking club princess. I didn't want to be looked after by thirty fucking bikers. The things I've done for this club, oh my God, the things I've done . . ." A sob escapes me, and I rub at the spot in my chest that aches. "You have no idea. You men think this club is here because of everything you all do to keep it here, but us women, we have a part to play too, and for you to dismiss it like I'm a spoilt brat who stalked you . . . I was a teenager, for Christ's sake. It was years ago. You made the first move and kissed me last week, and we were both in that room and both fucking."

Cammie lets out a scream and rushes towards me. She slaps me hard across the cheek, trying to grab my hair. I've been brought up around bikers, that shit doesn't slide with me, so I grip her by the throat. He cheated on her, so he's the one she should be slapping. Gunner gets between us, and there's a thud of heavy footsteps as Brick runs towards us and grabs me, pulling me away. I see Gunner hugging Cammie and checking her neck, and I store the image in my memory so I can use it to remind myself what a bastard he is.

CHAPTER EIGHT

Gunner

Cammie sits on my bed, her back against the wall, her arms folded, and a stony look on her face. She's been up here since the fight with Ava. I had to go about my duty, continuing to schmooze with the locals before Damien finally felt sorry for me and let me escape.

I feel the hatred and anger pouring from her. I begin to get undressed, occasionally glancing at her. "Are we gonna talk, darlin', or are you just gonna glare at me and ignore me? Cos I gotta tell yah, I'm not in the mood for another argument tonight."

"You fucked her. I was sitting next door, talking and making friends with these dumb, stupid fucking women who follow their bikers around like lovesick puppies, and you were in there fucking her!" She picks up a hardback book from her side of the bed and throws it, almost hitting my head.

"Jesus, Cameron, calm the fuck down. You're being dramatic."

She lets out a crazed scream and launches a glass towards me. It misses and shatters against the wall behind my head, scattering across the room. I dive at her and pin her to the bed, wrestling to hold her still.

"I messed up, I'm sorry, but I can't change it now," I huff out. She fights me, bucking and kicking out, but I get her pinned securely, halting her movements. I bend close to her ear. "This has to stop. You're my ol' lady now, and we have to move forward."

"You have to be kidding me. I am not yours. Fuck your ol' lady bullshit."

I let out a low, threatening laugh. "You ain't going nowhere, sweetheart. I've said sorry, it's done." I get up from her. "You launch anything else at my head and I'll tie you up for the night. Don't think I won't."

Cammie grabs the quilt and pulls it over her, laying down and turning away from me. Sulking, I can handle, so I get into bed. I lay behind her and hook an arm around her waist, pulling her towards me and wrapping myself around her.

I don't sleep straight away. Thoughts of Ava and Michael float around my head. There's a story there, and I want to know what it is and how it affects this club. I need to speak to Damien first thing.

I wake early the next morning and decide to go for a run. I need to clear my head before I speak to Damien.

By the time I return, Ava is up and dressed and sitting next to Evie, who's watching that stupid spoilt pig show on her iPad with headphones in.

"Thanks for last night, Ava. You really screwed things up with me and Cammie," I hiss. I know it isn't all her fault, that I shouldn't have put my dick in her, but I'm pissed off. She completely ignores me and it aggravates me further. "It hasn't worked. I'm staying with Cammie. I love her."

"Michael is Evie's father," she mutters, not taking her eyes from the iPad screen.

I feel like I've been punched in the gut and it takes me a minute to fully process her words.

"Michael?" I repeat. She doesn't reply. "Ava, you and him? When . . . how . . . why?"

When she still doesn't reply, I kick at the small table nearest to me, sending a couple glasses and the chairs surrounding it flying across the room. Ava jumps, covering Evie with her arms automatically. "For goodness' sake, Gunner, not in front of Evie," she hisses.

"You drop shit like that and expect me to do what? Shrug it off? Evie is my fucking niece, and I didn't even know. You fucked that scumbag? No wonder you kept that a secret. Keep your whore arse away from me. I can't even look at you right now." Ava bites her lower lip. I can see hurt in her eyes, but there are no tears this time. It's almost like she's flicked a switch and has no emotion.

I storm to my bedroom and shove the door open, causing it to bang against the wall. Cammie sits up suddenly, looking around dazed for the noise that woke her. "Marry me," I say seriously.

Cammie laughs and then realises I'm serious and freezes. "No, Ashton. You cheated on me and then lied about it."

I kick out of my joggers and pull my T-shirt over my head. "I'll spend the rest of my life making it up to you, I promise. I'm all yours from this day on." I crawl across the bed, moving over her sleepy body and settling between her legs.

She sighs. "Ashton, you can't fuck an answer out of me."

"Marry me."

I prod at her entrance, and she sucks in a breath. "No."

"Marry me."

I push into her slowly, and she groans. "No."

I nip at her bottom lip as I move in and out, the slow friction making her arch her back. I hold her wrists above her head and begin to move faster, chasing my orgasm. "You will marry me," I insist. "I'm not giving up."

Once Cammie's left for work, I head back down to the main room. Damien is with Evie. "Where's Ava?" I ask.

"She had a shift. Things okay with you and Cammie?" he asks, handing Evie over to Gemma.

I shrug, flopping down on the couch opposite him. I want to tell him about Ava and Michael, but I can't bring myself to. The words are still flying around my head like an annoying buzz. "I asked Cammie to marry me." I sigh, running a hand over my forehead.

"What? First, you're claiming her in front of the club, and now, you want to marry her?"

I smirk. "It's been a crazy few days."

"Look, is something going on between you and Ava?" I start to protest, but he holds his hand up to stop me. "Don't insult me, Gunner, we've been brothers for too long. I see it. This spontaneous shit with Cammie, is it because you're trying to forget whatever you had with Ava?" I don't speak, and after a minute or two, he sighs. "I just want you to know that if there was anything with you two, it would be okay with me. I wanna see you both happy. Life's too short."

Damien stands and heads to his office, leaving me gobsmacked. I wasn't expecting him to give his blessing. Ava means everything to Damien, and she's always been a priority for him. Out of all the guys, I would've thought he'd want her to be with someone with less bad history. Not that it matters now because Ava destroyed any chance of us this morning by uttering those words. I have so many questions, but fuck if I'm ready to face the truth.

Maddocks sits in the chair that Damien vacated. "What's up, buttercup?" He grins, popping a biscuit into his mouth, and I scowl at him. "What? You look like a guy with the weight of the world on his shoulders. Trouble in paradise already?"

"I wouldn't even know where to start, man." I sigh. "Ava told me something that's messed with my head."

Despite Maddocks' quick temper and terrible sense of humour, he's been a good friend for the last fifteen years. He joined the club after being in prison for a short time with Pops. Pops was still the Pres then, doing time for assault, and Maddocks was in for the same thing. They shared a cell, and Pops talked him into joining the MC. Maddocks reckons Pops saved his life, that if it wasn't for his intervention, he would've gone down a much darker path.

"Yeah? What'd she tell you?" he asks, leaning forward.

I stand. "Not here, brother. Let's go somewhere quiet."

We turn our bikes into the car park at Emzie's. "Anything progressing between you and Emma?" I ask as we enter the bar.

He shoots me a pissed-off look. "She drives me insane. She keeps going on dates with guys."

"Then ask her out," I suggest.

"I'm not ready for that. Why can't fucking just be enough? Why does she have to have a label on it?"

I laugh, shaking my head. Poor Emma didn't know what she signed up for the day she slept with Maddocks. He's a crazy bastard who refuses to be tamed but also refuses to let a woman go once he's decided he likes her. I'm pretty certain he's had restraining orders against him in the past.

Emma approaches us as we seat ourselves in a booth near the back. "What can I get you both?" she asks politely, like we're all strangers.

"Don't pull that bullshit, Queeny. I was balls deep in you last night, now you're gonna act like yah don't know me?"

"Jesus, Maddocks, don't start the minute you walk in here," she huffs. "I have customers."

I look at the two customers she's referring to. They haven't even looked up from their quiet conversation. "Two coffees is fine, thanks," I say.

Once she's gone, Maddocks leans in closer to me. "Come on then."

"Evie is my niece."

I watch closely as he absorbs this new information, and I see the moment he clicks all the pieces into place because his eyes practically bug out of his head. "No fucking way!"

"Don't tell anyone else. It ain't common knowledge, and I don't know what to do with it yet."

He nods in understanding. "How the hell did that happen? We would have noticed if she had a guy on the scene, especially Michael."

"I've been asking myself the same damn question all morning. It makes no sense."

Back when Ava was still in college, she was always picked up and dropped off. Damien was much more possessive when she was younger. Then she went to Uni, but that was miles away from home, so she stayed at the campus. For her to see Michael, she would've had to sneak out, unless he was turning up at Uni.

"Where does that leave the club? Does Michael know he's got a kid?" asks Maddocks.

I shrug. "I don't think so. He spoke to us at the barbeque and acted like he didn't know the kid. He asked if Ava and I were together and if the kid was mine."

"Damien is gonna shit a brick. Is she gonna tell him?"

"I haven't spoken to her about it. She told me this morning, and I was too pissed at her. I said some mean shit and then stormed off and asked Cammie to marry me." I groan and bury my face in my hands. "The shitter of it all is Damien gave me his blessing to be with Ava."

Maddocks arches an eyebrow. "Hold on, you like her?" He scratches his head in confusion. "I thought it was her who liked you."

"We have a small history. It's complicated." I brush it off and quickly change the subject.

Emma places a pot of black coffee on the table and two cups. "This looks like a deep conversation."

"Are you free tonight, Queeny?" asks Maddocks.

"Stop calling me that, and no, I'm seeing Ava tonight."

"Have a word with her, would yah," I say. "She's causing me all kinds of grief with Cammie."

Emma gives me an unapologetic look. "That's what happens when you screw her in the office while your wifey is in the next room."

Maddocks glares between us. "What the hell did I miss?" he asks me, then turns to Emma and asks, "And why didn't you tell me?"

"Because you said you didn't want to hear about any Ava-Gunner drama because it wasted our time together," she snaps.

Gunner laughs. "True, Queeny, I did say that."

"You want some advice, Gunner? Get your head out of your arse and claim the right woman. It was written in the stars, you and Ava," says Emma.

"No way. She moved on years ago when she had a kid with someone else," I snap.

"Because you broke her goddamn heart, Gunner. She was a mess back then. Not that it worked—the girl is crazy in love with you, and you treat her like shit."

"Everyone is always sticking up for Ava. What about the shit she's caused me?" I demand.

Emma rolls her eyes. "World's smallest violin on its way to you, Gunner," she says sarcastically. Once she's gone back to serving her customers, I turn back to Maddocks.

"So, do I tell Pres or let her do it? Either way, it's gonna impact the club. Is Michael back because of Ava? Were they together back then? There's too many unanswered questions."

Maddocks sips his coffee, the cup looking tiny in his huge hands. "You need to tell D. She's in danger if Michael finds out that Evie is his. If she'd have been claimed, it wouldn't have raised questions."

The words sit heavy with me. Maybe it was all my fault. I hurt her and pushed her into the arms of someone else. She's been paying for that ever since, and now Michael is back, what does that mean for her and Evie?

CHAPTER NINE

Ava

"How did you convince Rooster to let you out?" I ask Gemma as she slides the tray of drinks onto the table.

We all decided to get out of the clubhouse together and go to a bar across town. It's busy, but there isn't a biker in sight. We told Damien we were going to Emzie's, and he was sending a guy to follow us after they finished in church. He took his eye off the ball, and we snuck off. The guys will go insane when they realise we aren't there, but by then, we will hopefully be so drunk that we won't care.

"With a good blowjob and the promise of a night of passion. See the sacrifices I make for you, girl?" She grins.

I laugh. "Sorry, I owe you one."

"So, what's going down with you and Gunner?" asks Chloe.

"Yeah, he told me to have a word with you for fucking with his relationship," adds Emma.

The girls don't know about Michael. I couldn't explain back then what was going on, and I feel bad, but after I got pregnant, they never asked me about the father. They knew I was getting enough shit about it from Damien, and to be honest, I think they thought it was Gunner.

"I told her about us sleeping together the other day." They all stare at me open-mouthed. "I know, okay, it was a shit move."

"What's going on with you lately? Since Gunner came back, you've been acting crazy," says Chloe, topping up our glasses with the leftover wine.

"I can't explain it. I'm a bitch and I totally deserve to be bitch-slapped, but I'm so sick of him treating me like some psycho stalker. He made the move in the office and he's the one attached, not me, so theoretically, I didn't do anything wrong because I wasn't the one cheating."

"Ava, don't be that girl," groans Gemma. "You knew about Cammie."

"You're all supposed to be on my side. You're supposed to hate her."

"We love you, baby girl, but you have to move on. Gunner doesn't want you, he chose her," says Emma gently, patting my hand. I drink my wine in two gulps, placing the empty glass down.

"Thanks," I grumble. "I can always count on you three to lift me up."

"Do you want us to lie, encourage you to keep on this path with a dead end? At what point will you realise Gunner's not yours? He never was. He's slept with you twice and broke your heart both times," says Emma.

Tears fill my eyes and Chloe wraps her arm around my shoulders. "We love you, Ava. We want you to be happy, but that ship has well and truly sailed."

"I need more wine," I sniffle, wiping my eyes on a napkin.

Emma stands. "Wine and shots, coming up."

We're almost through the second bottle of wine when Gemma's mobile buzzes along the wooden table.

"Hey, baby. You took your time." She holds the phone away from her ear, wincing, and then she stands and whispers to us that she can't hear too well, so she heads outside.

"I want someone to call me and worry," I say, "other than my brother."

A minute later, Gemma dashes back inside, holding her phone to her chest. "Get your shit together, we have to go."

We all stand, saving our questions, and gather our bags and jackets. As we exit the booth, Chloe halts, causing me to crash into her back. "Chlo," I screech.

"Isn't that Cammie?" she asks, pointing over to the far side of the bar. It's really busy, so it takes me a second to see Cammie standing by the bathroom doors.

"Yeah. Is Gunner here?" I ask. The other two have already gone, so Chloe begins to lead us out. When I look back towards Cammie, it's in time to see her sucking face with a tall, broad guy . . . who's not Gunner.

We get outside into the fresh air and catch up with Emma and Gemma. "Where's the fire?" I ask. "I saw something really important in there."

"Rooster hit the roof, said that bar is Saints territory now. Apparently, it's part of a deal with your brother that's just gone down."

Damien usually tells me what bars to avoid. Being caught in there would not have gone down well with the rival club.

"Listen, Chlo and I saw Cammie and . . ." My words fade when a car pulls up, Rooster at the wheel.

"Get in the fucking car now," he yells.

We all pile in. "Sorry, we didn't know," says Gemma as she gets in the front.

"I am way too pissed to talk to you right now, so shut the fuck up," orders Rooster.

We all sit in silence. There's no point in pushing his buttons, he'll only explode, and he won't be the angriest—Damien will be far more pissed.

When we get back to the club, the engine doesn't even cut off before Damien is ripping the door open and dragging Chloe out.

"What is it about you fucking bitches and rules?" he roars as we pile out of the car. "You could have gotten yourselves killed tonight. You think the Saints are like us? You think they'll think twice about slitting your damn throat or raping you?"

I sigh. "Relax, Damien, we're fine."

"And you . . . you're causing me enough shit right now. I'm close to packing you the fuck off to Spain with Ma and Pops."

"I'm not a kid, Damien."

He gets close to my face, making me flinch. "Push me once more, Ava, I'm not kidding. This is my club, and I don't have the time or manpower to follow you around at the minute because you can't follow simple goddamn fucking instructions," he shouts.

"I'm an adult! I can look after myself," I yell.

Damien backs me to the car, towering over me in a menacing stance. "All you seem to do at the minute is cause problems. Keep your head down and do as you're told, or I swear, you're on the next plane. Twenty-four fucking years old and I'm still watching over you. Sort yourself out and get yourself a man, so I can pass on the responsibility to some other mug," he yells. I push past him, noticing the gathering crowd watching us. "And leave my VP and his ol' lady alone," he barks after me. "Ol' ladies come above unattached pains in the arse."

Once I get inside, I make my way to the bar. Tap hands me a vodka, and I throw it back, slamming the glass on the bar top for another refill. Pops takes a seat next to me.

"He's got a lot on, Ava. You're only adding to his stress," says Pops.

"Fine, I'll be the perfect little sister. He won't hear a peep out of me."

Pops rolls his eyes. "Yah know, all you had to do was settle down, have a family, and live happily ever after. We made it easy for you. Your brother took on this club and he's responsible for everyone in it—families, the kids, the guys. He isn't kidding about Spain, though. He asked your ma if she'd consider moving back out there with you and Evie for a few months."

"Well, maybe I'll consider going just to get away from him," I mutter.

"Lie low for a while, he'll calm down," Pops advises before leaving me in peace.

I get a text message, and when I see it's from Michael, I groan aloud. That's all I need to finish my day off. It's his demand to see me for the DNA test. I have no idea how the hell I'm going to get out of this place after tonight.

I look up from my phone when Damien storms in with Chloe on his heels, trying to talk to him. He ignores her and goes into his office, slamming the door in her face. She heads towards me, rejection clear in her eyes. "Welcome to my world," I joke, and she half smiles.

"I can't understand him. He acts like my husband only without any of the sex or interaction," she huffs, snatching my vodka and drinking it.

"Tap, you may as well pass us the bottle," I suggest, and he hands it to us with an extra glass for Chloe.

"Cammie was kissing someone who wasn't Gunner," I say, and she slams her glass down.

"What? Who?"

"I don't know, but I think he had a kutte on. I couldn't see the back properly, but if it's Saints territory . . ."

"You need to go and tell Damien," she says. "He needs to know that."

"After the way he just went off?" She gives me her serious face, and I groan. "Fine."

I knock on the office door. "What?" comes Damien's agitated voice.

I push the door open, and he glares at me as I enter. "Sorry to bother you, Pres," I say, my voice dripping in sarcasm. He raises his eyebrows in warning. "I saw Cammie tonight. She was at that bar." He stares at me, no expression on his face. "She was kissing a guy in a kutte, and I think it might have been a Saint."

"And it was definitely her? Because I swear, if you're making this shit up to come between Gunner and—"

"Thanks for your faith in me, Damien. Is that how little you think of me?"

"I don't even know you at the moment, Ava. You're fucking Gunner under my nose and sneaking about in places you don't belong. What do I do when you disrespect an ol' lady? If you were a club girl, you'd be out."

"But I'm not. Look, if you want me out, then just say and I'll go to Spain. But it was Cammie, and he wasn't Gunner." I leave the office and re-join Chloe. "He asked if I was lying," I tell her.

"Ouch. He's really pissed off," says Chloe. "Gunner just got back, if you want to tell him."

I laugh. "Not a chance. He called me a whore today, so I don't owe him fuck all."

I feel his eyes on me as he sits at the bar watching me. Eventually, he makes his way over. "Give us a minute, Chloe," he mutters. She gives me an apologetic look before leaving, then he sits down. "I need some answers."

"Okay."

"Does Michael know about Evie?" I give a nod, and he utters a string of curse words. "Does he want to see her?"

I nod again. "He only just found out. He's insisting on a DNA test, but I think he'll try to take her from me."

He puts his face in his hands. "You have to tell Damien."

I shake my head. "No way. He hates me right now and wants to send me to Spain. Once the DNA test is back, I may as well just go. Michael will make my life hell."

Gunner seems to ponder this for a minute and then shrugs. "It might be for the best. Things aren't really going well here for you."

"That would be ideal for you, wouldn't it? You have sex with me, and somehow, I'm taking the brunt of the blame. Typical fucking man."

"I ain't arguing with you anymore, Ava. You need to tell Damien, or I will. This might affect the club. If you go, Michael might take it out on the club, and if you stay, he might take Evie. You need Pres' help on this one."

I know I need to come clean, but the thought of disappointing Pops and Damien further has me considering ways to get out of it. I wish I hadn't told Gunner. "I'll think about it. While we're talking about honesty, I need to tell you something. I saw Cammie tonight in a bar across town. She was kissing another man."

He clenches his jaw in that pissed-off, brooding way he does. "I don't believe you."

"Well, it's true. The bar was in Saints territory. I told Damien." He stands abruptly and marches to the office.

Chloe re-joins me. "Why do our nights out always end in drama?" she asks. I laugh because she's right—something always happens and we always end up back here at the clubhouse, drinking house vodka and contemplating our lives.

"I've decided to give Damien an ultimatum," Chloe announces. Damien hates being backed into a corner.

"About the two of you?" I ask, and she nods. "Chloe, I'm not sure he'll give you the answer you're looking for."

"I know. I can't live like this anymore, though, so I'm laying it all on the line, and then if he can't be honest and admit how he feels, that's it, I'm done. I'll move on and not look back."

"Wish I was as strong-minded as you," I mutter, watching Gunner come out of Damien's office on his mobile. A minute later, Cammie appears and rushes over to him, kissing him hard on the mouth. I exchange a confused look with Chloe. Clearly, she doesn't know we saw her or that Gunner knows.

He smiles and whispers something in her ear. She laughs and then he takes her hand and leads her upstairs. "Well, clearly, he chose to believe her over me."

"What did you expect after everything that's gone down recently? He probably thinks you're trying to split them up."

Chloe's right, it looks like I'm trying to cause trouble. I decide to take a step back. Gunner needs to sort his own life out, and I have a certain ghost from the past to deal with. When the DNA confirms Michael as Evie's father, I'm screwed. The thought sends my stomach into knots. Maybe Damien sending me off to Spain isn't a bad thing, and I decide to give it serious thought.

The following day, I wake Evie early. Michael wants us to meet him at his office, which is a forty-minute drive.

We have breakfast and then we get dressed and head for the car. Damien isn't up yet, and none of the guys are about, so I'll be able to leave without much trouble. It's when I return that I'll get the lecture.

I strap Evie into her car seat and close the door. When I look up, Gunner is standing close by, watching me, and I jump in fright. "Christ, why are you sneaking around?"

"Where are you sneaking off to?" he asks suspiciously.

"I have shit to do, Gunner. Stay out of my business."

I head around to the driver's side, and he follows me. "You need to tell Damien, Ava. I'm serious about this." I pull the door open, but he slams his hand against it, closing it. "Ava, Michael is trouble. You have to have Damien on side if you're taking him on."

"I'll sort it out. I got myself into this mess and I don't need you bikers making everything crazy. Besides, if things get heated, I'll take the offer to go to Spain. Michael won't follow me there when he's got the opportunity to mess with you here."

"If you don't tell Damien today, I will. And where are you going without an escort?"

My phone beeps pulling my attention away from Gunner. It's Michael asking if I've set off. "Look, I have to go, Gunner. Your brother is demanding my attention."

He balls his fists. "What? He calls, and you go running?" he asks bitterly, dropping his arm to his side. I pull the car door open and climb inside.

"I'm sorry you hate me and that I've disappointed you so much, but you've made it perfectly clear that we're nothing to each other, not even friends, so please keep out of my business."

I slam the door and start the engine, watching him in the rear-view mirror as I drive away.

I make it in record time to Michael's offices. There's security in the main reception, so I give my name and they buzz through to Michael, who soon appears looking as smarmy as ever in his suit and tie.

"Let's get this shitshow over with." He appears cold, like I don't belong in this building or with him, and he doesn't bother to acknowledge Evie.

I follow him into a huge office. There's one desk by a window overlooking the city and then a bar area towards the back of the room. A blonde lady is sitting on a couch with a box of toys at her feet. She looks kind and smiles at Evie. There's also a tall, thin man standing with a briefcase by the desk.

"This is Cole, my lawyer. He's got the DNA test. And that's Ursula. She works in the office but will be helping me out with Evelyn whenever I have her over, which will be all the time once the results come back."

Ursula gives Evie a small wave and holds up a Barbie doll. Evie leads me over by the hand, eager to play with all the new shiny toys. "I thought the toys might distract her while she has her swabs done," says Ursula, smiling.

"Thanks," I mutter. I'm grateful someone seems to care about my daughter's welfare.

"Ava, come and sign these papers," Michael orders. I leave Evie with Ursula and approach the desk. The man hands me a form giving my consent to the test, and I sign it.

The test is done within minutes. Cole tells me it could take up to two weeks for it to return, but he'll contact me directly with the results. He'll also send me a copy of the results in the post, so I can have someone look over them if I have any concerns. I'm already sure that Michael is the father because he always refused to use protection. My phone buzzes, and I glance down to see Damien's name flash across the screen.

"Is that your brother wondering where his club princess is?" mocks Michael.

"If we're finished here, I have to go. He'll be pissed if I don't answer."

"Then answer." He grins, taking a seat behind his desk.

I sigh and connect the call. "Yes, Damien?"

"After everything we said, you go and leave with Evie and you don't take an escort or tell me where you're going?"

He sounds surprisingly calm, but I know that's just because he's building up to it. "I'll explain when I get back, okay. I'm sorry, Damien." I disconnect the call.

Cole leaves, and Michael indicates for me to sit in the chair opposite him. I glance at Evie, who's happily playing with Ursula. "When the results come back, you have a choice to make," says Michael.

"I do?"

He nods. "I don't want my daughter growing up in some hellhole biker dump. How you can call yourself a good mother and then leave your daughter to live like that is beyond me. So, either you move her to this side of town—I'll get you a house—or you can sign her over to me."

I laugh. I knew he'd try to pull a stunt, but this is ridiculous. "Not happening."

"Ava, don't be so stupid. I'm the chief of police. What judge is going to let you keep her? By the time I've painted the picture of the club whore who drinks too much and parties hard, you'll be lucky if you even get contact. I'm a respected upstanding citizen, a concerned father, and you, well, you're just a club princess still living with her brother and about thirty other men."

"I'm an upstanding citizen too. I'm a nurse, and I don't drink and party too much."

Michael reaches into his desk drawer, the mahogany creaking as he pulls it open. He places a folder on the table in front of him and takes out some photos. He lays them carefully one by one in front of me, and I gasp. There's pictures of me from nights out, holding glasses of vodka or gin, drinking shots, hanging around the necks of club members. He's been through my social media accounts and printed these off.

"I'm allowed a life, Michael. My mum cares for Evie when I'm not there," I argue.

He shrugs, gathering his photos up and placing them back into the folder. "Depends what the judge sees, doesn't it?"

"No judge will believe that."

"Maybe, maybe not, but are you willing to take the risk? Judge Kennedy is fantastic with family law, favours fathers who work hard and play good golf. We often eat at his mansion, and he has a lovely holiday home in France. I can't wait to take Evelyn."

Tears spring to my eyes and I blink them away. "Evie, we have to go." She runs to me, gripping my hand.

"I'll be in touch at the weekend. I'd like a visit with Evelyn, get to know her."

"Not until the results are back," I snap.

I march from the office, and my hands shake as I press the call button for the elevator. "Mummy, are you kay?" asks Evie, smiling up at me.

I nod, forcing myself to return her smile. Gunner's right, I need to tell Damien.

When I get back to the clubhouse, I find Gunner sitting at the bar, Cammie by his side. "You're in so much shit, Ava," he remarks as I pass.

"Don't I know it," I mutter.

I find Mum sitting at the table in the kitchen, chopping vegetables. "Hey, Mum, any chance you could watch Evie? I need to talk to Damien."

She smiles at Evie. "Of course, Are you both okay? He was yelling and cursing so much earlier, even Gunner was surprised."

"It's my fault, I'll sort it now."

I knock on Damien's office door. "What?" he yells.

I pop my head around the door and find Chloe is standing in front of Damien. "Sorry, I'll come back," I say.

"No, it's fine, we're done," mutters Chloe. She makes a move and Damien grabs her arm, but she pulls herself free. "Don't," she warns.

Once she's gone, his glare turns from soft to angry. "I have tickets for your flight to Spain on my computer. If this excuse is bullshit, I'm confirming them with you standing here."

"I went to see Evie's father." He freezes, his mouth half open. "I need your help, Pres." And for once, I'm not being sarcastic.

CHAPTER TEN

Gunner

I can't help but keep glancing at the office door. Ava went in there over an hour ago to speak with Damien. I haven't spoken to him since last night when we discussed Cammie and her cheating arse.

I watch Cammie tapping away on her mobile and refrain from snatching it to see who the fuck she's texting. She looks up, feeling my eyes on her, and smiles. "You okay?" she asks.

I nod, not wanting to give the game away. Damien believes Ava, and if I'm honest, so do I. She wouldn't lie about something like that. Damien wants me to keep up the happy couple act to see what she's up to while he does some digging to see if anyone knows anything about her.

The office door finally opens and Damien pops his head out. He looks less stressed and angry. "VP, get in here." I give Cammie a kiss on the head, noting how she moves her phone to her chest.

"Yes, Pres."

Damien closes the door behind me. Ava is sitting on a stool, her face red and her eyes puffy from crying. The need to hold her is overwhelming, so I sit on the couch and fold my arms, not trusting myself around her.

"I'll get to how pissed I am with you later," says Damien, pointing to me. There's no point in arguing with him when he has that dangerous glint in his eye. "We need a plan. Michael wants Evie, and I'll fucking die before that happens."

I'm relieved that Ava's told Damien. I didn't want to be the one to break that news to him.

"Michael doesn't have a clue about kids. I'm sure he's just stirring shit," I say, trying to sound unaffected.

"He knows some hotshot judge and he sounds very confident. He even printed off photos of me out drinking with the girls to build a bad picture of me," says Ava, tears welling in her eyes again.

I shrug. "So, go to Spain. Take Evie so he can't find her."

Damien gives me a look that says 'stop the bull'. "You happy that your dick of a brother is gonna take our niece? Or that I might have to send them both away to a foreign country?"

"He's not my fuckin' brother, Pres. And no, of course, I ain't, but I also ain't happy that she fucked him in the first place."

"Everyone makes mistakes, and besides, that's not the problem right now. We have a bigger issue. He's threatened Ava, told her she's got to move to a condo that he'll put her up in or else he's taking Evie."

I stand, pacing back and forth. That little fucker. "What's he got on you?"

Ava shrugs. "Just those pictures, I think."

"Then I don't know what you're gonna do. I don't think moving will solve it. It might give you more time, but if he files for custody in your absence, they'll order that you return."

"We need to call church," Damien says. "I need someone on you all the time, Ava. I mean it, no sneaking off, especially not to meet him. He calls, you tell me, and we'll get you out to him without him knowing we're there. Let's keep him sweet until we find a way out of this."

Ava nods. "Thanks, Damien." She stands and gives him a hug. The short top she wears with her leggings rises as she stretches up to him, and her smooth skin teases me.

Once she's left the office, I turn to Damien. "I'll be on her," I say before I've fully thought it through.

"You can't be. We have shit with Cammie to deal with, and she'll lose her shit if I put you on the woman you cheated on her with."

"This is more important. You know I'll protect her and you know she won't give me the slip."

"I don't think she'll give us the slip again. She knows this is serious. I don't want Evie leaving this building, not even if he requests it," says Damien.

I agree. Who knows what Michael is capable of. There's a knock on the door and Maddocks looks in, "Sorry, Pres, but we have a situation. That prick's here, Michael."

We groan in unison. "Did he say what he wants?" I ask.

"Just to see the Pres."

"Send him in." Damien sighs. "Let's see if he tells us exactly what he wants."

I sit down facing Damien, and he lowers into his large office chair, placing his boot-clad feet onto his desk, giving the impression we're relaxed.

Maddocks shows Michael in. "Afternoon, gentlemen."

I settle for a nod because I want to beat the fuck out of the bastard and I don't trust myself to speak. Damien stands and leans over his desk to shake his hand. I don't know how he does that when he's just found out what happened between him and Ava.

"To what do we owe this pleasure?"

"Just thought I'd check in, see how you guys were all doing."

"Sure, yah did," I mutter.

"Did Ava get back okay? Not sure I like how easy she gets away from you guys," he says, and I realise he wants to throw Ava under the bus as well as piss us off. He's trying to cause ripples between us.

"Yea, she got back just fine. She's a big girl. But that's nice of you to come and check on my sister," says Damien.

"Soon to be my wife, if I have my way," Michael drops in, picking up a picture of Evie and Ava from Damien's desk.

"That ain't ever happening," I growl, gripping the arm rests of the chair to prevent me from diving up and beating the shit out of him.

"We'll see. She's gotta be lonely with no husband, a kid on her own. When I show her what a normal family lives like, she might realise what a bunch of shitheads you really are."

"Can we help you with anything else today, Officer? We have shit to do," says Damien, calm and relaxed.

"Did Ava tell you why she came to see me today?" asks Michael, looking smug.

"Of course, she did, Michael. We're her family, she tells us everything. That's how families work. Oh, crap, sorry, forgot you don't have a family," says Damien.

Michael scowls and then seems to shrug it off. "I want to see Evie."

"That isn't happening until you have your test results," Damien says firmly.

"Get Ava. It's up to her."

Damien sighs but gets up and leans out the office door, shouting for Ava. When she comes in, she freezes. She obviously didn't know he was here.

"I want to see Evie and these clowns think you'll have a problem with that," Michael says with a smirk.

Ava glances at Damien for guidance. "I'd prefer you didn't, Michael, until we know for sure. It might confuse her."

"Fuck that, you know she's mine. Get her."

I stand, pissed off with this bullshit. "Get the fuck out. She said no."

Michael gives me an amused look and then tilts his head towards Ava. Her face changes, like she's panicking, and she goes towards Michael. "Why don't you come and talk to me instead?" She pulls him from the room.

We follow her out, but she waves her hand at us, a false smile telling us she's not okay but we shouldn't intervene.

"That was weird," I say, and Damien nods. We both watch them disappear upstairs. "Should we intervene?"

"No, she's trying to keep him sweet. Let her do this, and we can call church and try and get him out of her life for good."

Ava

"What do you want, Michael? I did your stupid test. You can't show up at my home just to piss the guys off." I take him into a spare room on the second floor. It has a couch and a television but nothing else. I didn't want to risk taking him in to a room with a bed and giving him the wrong idea.

"It's going to be a new hobby of mine, Ava. Turn up, piss them off, fuck their princess, and so on." He grins.

"You're goading the wrong people, Michael. There're thirty pissed-off bikers who live here, and they all hate your guts. If you keep pissing them off, they won't give a fuck that you're in the police."

"I'm not just in the police, princess, I'm the top of the police. I can fuck this club up and you know it. I don't even need the evidence I already have to do that."

I cross my arms, goosebumps breaking out across my skin, and suddenly, I feel cold. Michael steps towards me, hooking his finger around one of mine and tugging me until I step forward.

"It's been a few years since I've felt the way your pussy grips my cock."

When I don't respond, his hand flies up to my throat and he grips it tight, causing me to gasp for breath. "Please, not here, Michael," I cough out.

He reaches over and drops the lock on the door. Reaching into his pocket, he pulls out his mobile phone and opens a video. I don't need to open my eyes to see it—he's shown it to me so many times, I know every detail.

"Open your fucking eyes and watch it," he growls, squeezing tighter.

I open in time to see a younger-looking Damien and Gunner beating the shit out of Al Monteo.

"Do it," orders Damien, his voice firm.

Gunner steps back as Al falls to the floor, groaning. He isn't dead yet, but then Gunner pulls out a gun and puts a bullet in his head. It's quick, and Al's body jumps as the impact of the bullet hits him and then the groans stop. The footage is wobbly, filmed from a distance by someone hiding, but it's clear who's there and exactly who pulled the trigger and who ordered him to.

Michael lets go of my throat and takes a step back, smirking because he knows what comes next . . . and so do I. The next video plays out, and before he makes me watch that one too, I lift my top over my head and drop it to the floor. He gives a satisfied smile and tucks the phone away, folding his arms across his chest, watching with pleasure in his eyes. Once I'm completely naked, he backhands me across the face. I fall to the floor, and he gets a handful of my hair, pulling me to my knees. Fire burns my scalp as the roots cling on in protest. "Do not scream. If you alert those fuckers downstairs, you know what'll happen."

Michael unfastens his trousers and shoves them down his legs. "Get it wet," he orders, moving his hand up and down his hard shaft. He crams it into my mouth, making me wince, occasionally slapping my face. Once he feels he's about to climax, he pulls out and uses my hair to make me stand. "Touch your toes," he says as he pushes my shoulders.

I bend, hating that I'm vulnerable in this position. I feel the sting of his slap as he brings his hand down hard on my backside. I bite my lip to stop my yelp. He does it over and over, and then he's behind me, pressing his cock against the entrance to my ass. I hate anal sex, and he knows this. It's almost like he wants me to scream. He's always gotten off on pain.

He pushes in an inch at a time, groaning as he gets deeper. I close off my mind, thinking of Gunner. Even though he hates me right now, he's always the thought that takes me away from this, from him.

I feel like I'm about to vomit and then he finally comes. We've been here for almost twenty minutes and I'm not sure I can take much more pain. He suddenly pulls out and groans low as he spurts his release over my back. He slaps my arse one last time and then uses his hand to rub his release into my skin, like he's marking my flesh.

Once his breathing is slightly calmer, he presses his semi-hard cock against my opening and I want to scream. I was hopeful he'd be done. "Your turn. I want to hear you come, princess."

I bite my lip. That isn't going to happen . . . it never does. After two minutes, I scream out, faking my orgasm to satisfy his need. If I didn't, he'd just continue to try.

Michael takes his time sorting his clothes so he looks crisp and put together, like he did when he walked in over half an hour ago. I sit on the couch, trying my best to cover myself. If I dress before he leaves, he'll take it as defiance and is likely to make me undress again, which usually results in another fuck, and I can't put myself through that again. He leans down and kisses me on the forehead. "See you soon, baby."

He leaves, and I wonder if he even realises that what just happened between us was not normal, that I didn't want it. Because he always acts so normal, like we're lovers sneaking around.

As soon as the door closes, I lock it again and slide down it, tears falling uncontrollably. I press my face into my hands and cry into them to muffle the sound. I don't know what to do. I want to tell Damien, but Michael's threats are real. Everything is so messed up right now.

I jump when a knock on the door startles me out of the nightmare I've suddenly found myself in. "Open the fucking door, Ava."

It's Gunner and, as usual, he sounds angry with me. I wipe my face quick, hoping it isn't too red, and I wince as I stand. Being bent over for that long has taken its toll on my legs. Gunner is now kicking at the door impatiently, yelling my name. I grab my clothes and pull them on, then I yank the door open and put on my best annoyed face. He storms forward, causing me to stumble back.

"You fucked him," he states, looking me up and down.

I stutter. Of course, it's obvious what just happened between me and Michael, and I'm pretty sure Michael would have hinted at the fact as he left. I shrug like I'm not bothered what he thinks, yet inside, I'm screaming at him to see what's going on. "I need to shower. Is this gonna take long?" I snap.

Gunner's fist misses my face by an inch as it slams into my wall, plaster falling away and leaving a Hulk-sized hole. I stare at him open-mouthed. "There's something you aren't telling us. There's no way you'd fuck him willingly. I see the hate in your eyes," he yells. I sigh and push past him, needing to be away from his temper. I make my way to the bathroom as Gunner follows. "Yeah, you go and wash that slimy bastard from your skin. Shall I get you the bleach?"

I slam the door in his face and lock it, resting my head against the cold wood as tears begin to fall again.

Later, once Evie is asleep, I head downstairs. Chloe texted me after she spoke to Damien that she wants to talk. When I get down, I find Emma has joined her. They have a table in the corner, and I'm glad there aren't many people about.

I notice Gunner sitting in another corner of the room, watching me. He's taking his role as babysitter far too seriously. He even stood outside the bathroom while I showered, and he's ordered one of the prospects to stand outside the bedroom door while Evie sleeps.

"We're staging a friend-tervension," announces Chloe proudly as I take a seat. She points to a pot of hot coffee and the three cups. "Not even a drop of alcohol."

I roll my eyes, needing alcohol to get through this. I never told the girls about Michael, and now, I have to. "So, what's the friend-tervension for?" I ask, pouring a coffee and sipping it with distain.

"Like you don't know. Damien said you might need us tonight because Evie's father is back on the scene," says Chloe.

"Yeah, he's back."

"Do we have to drag it out of you?" snaps Emma.

"It's Michael, Gunner's brother."

They both stare at me and the silence grows uncomfortable. "I'm sorry . . . but what?" stutters Chloe.

I give a nod to confirm they heard me right, "It was a long time ago," I add with a shrug.

"But why? Why . . . I . . . erm . . ." Emma trails off, clearly at a loss for words.

"No," bursts out Chloe. "No, you hate him. You absolutely hate him. There is no way you'd sleep with him."

I smile gratefully at Chloe, thankful that at least she knows me well enough. It confirms what I already wanted to do—confide in them.

"It was after Gunner. I got drunk, I was sad and lonely, and he turned up looking for Gunner. You know how much I was hurting back then. It was a stupid mistake, but it gave me a beautiful daughter and I don't regret her."

"I don't understand. Was it punishment for Gunner hurting you? Fuck the brother he hates so much?" asks Emma.

I shrug. "Maybe. I can't really remember why or how it even happened, I was so drunk."

"And so now he's back and knows about Evie?" asks Chloe.

"Yeah. He wants me to move nearer him, or he's going to take Evie. He has photos of me, and they paint a picture of a drunk who doesn't care about her daughter."

"What a bastard," mutters Chloe.

I nod in agreement. The events of the day begin to catch up with me and tears pool in my eyes again. Chloe rushes to my side and pulls me into a hug.

"Damien will sort it all out. He won't let him take you or Evie."

"Chloe, it isn't that simple," I mutter.

She pulls back to look at me. "I knew there was more to this."

"Keep your face straight when I tell you this," I say, looking from Chloe to Emma. "I wasn't being completely honest just then. I didn't want to get back at Gunner by sleeping with Michael. He's blackmailing me . . . or he was. Well, I guess he still is. He has footage. It's of Al Monteo," I whisper.

Emma's eyes go wide at the mention of that name. "Shit."

"Why haven't you told Damien?" asks Chloe.

"Because he'll go in all guns blazing. Michael isn't stupid. He has others waiting to take that footage to the police. And that's not all he has. Before Al died, it seems he sent Michael the video of me..." I trail off, biting my lower lip.

"Oh, Ava," Choe cries quietly, her hand covering her mouth. "What the fuck are we gonna do?"

I smile at her words. The fact she uses 'we' and not 'you' means she has my back, and it's just what I needed to hear. "If I tell the guys, then that video goes to websites everywhere. Then he'll show the one of Al's murder to the police."

"Shit, shit, shit. There has to be a way around this. Why the hell didn't you tell us sooner, when this all first started?" demands Emma.

"I was scared. I didn't want anything bad to happen to Damien or Gunner. Then Michael just left, and I thought maybe that was the end to it all, that he'd gotten bored and moved on. When I saw he was back, I panicked. I have Evie to protect now. I know I should tell Damien all of it, but it will destroy him. He did everything to protect me, and now, I want to protect him. What if I tell them everything and then Michael not only uses those videos against us but files for parental rights over Evie? He knows a judge, and he has it all worked out."

"You have to tell Damien just so mean machine over there stops glaring at you like that. How do you not wilt? He is one scary motherfucker," says Chloe, nodding towards Gunner.

I look over in his direction, his stern glare still fixed on me. "He thinks I've willingly fucked his brother. I don't blame him."

"But you haven't. You did it to save his arse."

"I have two weeks at least until the DNA is back. Once it's in, I'll be moving with Evie closer to Michael. It's the only way."

Both girls protest, but I don't hear them over the beating of my heart. It thumps in my chest at the thought of being Michael's plaything until I can find a way out of all this. There is no way I can risk Evie. It's better that I'm with her than him taking her from me and me never seeing her again. I just can't take the risk.

I head to my room after the girls leave, both having promised to come up with a plan. It's nice that they're trying to help me, and I wish I'd told them sooner. But I know deep down there's only one way out of this, and that's to do whatever Michael wants.

I hear Gunner's footsteps behind me. "You don't have to follow me to bed."

"I'm sticking with you everywhere."

"I'm inside the clubhouse. I'm safe here."

"The Pres put me on you. I'm doing it for him, not you."

Gunner follows me into my room, grabbing himself a blanket from my drawers. He gets comfy on the chair in the corner, and I get into bed silently. It's hard to fall asleep with him sitting in the corner of the room, but somehow, I feel myself drifting.

CHAPTER ELEVEN

Gunner

The moaning gets louder, and I slowly open my eyes. Then the scream has me sitting up and rushing over to Ava. She's twisted in the sheet and crying in her sleep. Evie doesn't stir, which amazes me because Ava sounds pained. "No, stop! Al, stop!"

I freeze. I haven't heard that name for so long, it throws me for a second. She's dreaming about the attack by Al Monteo, a Spanish fucker who thought he could take Ava.

I gently reach out and stroke Ava's shoulder, but she slaps at my hands, crying harder.

"Ava, baby, it's me," I whisper, and she calms at my voice. "It's okay, darlin', I'm here."

I carefully get on the bed, spooning behind her, and she stills. Her crying stops and she turns to face me, snuggling against my chest and gripping my vest in her tiny shaking hand. I wrap her in my arms and place gentle kisses on her head. Thoughts of Al Monteo fill my mind and I wonder what's brought on these sudden nightmares. It must be Michael's reappearance that's unsettled her.

Ava was thirteen years old, a sassy teenager who thought she could take on the world. Her smart mouth often got her into trouble, not only with Pops and Damien but also in school. Not growing up in a normal house meant Ava had a bit more freedom than most teens her age. We had parties at the clubhouse most weekends, and Ava would often invite friends. I lost count of the amount of times Pops found her drunk. I smile at the memories.

Ava had asked to go to a party by a popular girl from her school, but Pops wasn't keen on the family, so he told her no. Of course, she took off without being seen and went anyway. We didn't realise it at the time, but she had been chatting to some kid on the internet and the party was a lie for her to get out. She was going to meet this kid at his house, only when she got there, it wasn't a kid. But it was a party . . . and Ava was the guest of honour.

You hear about these things, kids being sold and used for sex, but it shouldn't have happened to Ava, to our club, or in our town. By the time we realised she'd snuck out and had tracked her down, it was too late. He'd already taken what he couldn't give back. Ava was half-dead, tied up in a dirty barn in the middle of nowhere. It was lucky that Pops was so cautious and had put a tracker on her phone or we would never have found her alive.

I spend the rest of the night wide awake and huddled next to Ava. I know she doesn't talk about any of that, she dealt with it, but I wonder if she's been having nightmares about that time all along.

The next morning, I feel Ava pull away gently, trying not to wake me. I lay still, pretending to be asleep. I can't face her analysing why I'm lying next to her still. I just wanted to settle her. But despite her nightmare, I'm still pissed at her. She acted like she wasn't pleased to see Michael and then she fucked him—none of it makes sense. Maybe having a kid with someone gives you that deeper connection, or maybe she's trying to keep him sweet so he doesn't take Evie.

She creeps out of the room, and I roll onto my back. Evie is still sleeping next to me, and her light snores make me smile. She doesn't deserve any of this, and that just pisses me off further.

I lay there for some time, trying to get my thoughts together. Damien put a guy on trying to find out who the fuck Cammie is, but I've heard nothing and that shit is grating on me. Trying to pretend she's my ol' lady is hard work when all I want to do is slit her damn throat.

Evie rolls over and crawls to my side. She lets out a cry, and I pull her onto my chest, where she settles quickly, her arms and legs sprawled across me, as I gently stroke her back. She smells like Ava, and it aches my heart. The bedroom door opens and Ava stops dead in her tracks, staring at the scene before her, then she bolts out the door again without saying a word.

Evie wakes about ten minutes later and grins at me with a cute sleepy look on her face. "Morning, sleepyhead. Should we go and find Mummy?" She nods, rubbing her eyes sleepily as I lift her and carry her downstairs. Ava is sitting by the window, staring into space. I hand Evie to her, and she snaps out of her daydream, taking her daughter and kissing her on her head.

"Damien rang into work for me, told them I was really sick and couldn't come in for a while."

I nod, grabbing myself a bottle of water. "Well, looks like we're staying at the clubhouse today."

She sighs. "I think I'll be spending a lot of time here."

Ava predicted right. The next week is spent at the clubhouse, and time passes slowly, every painstaking minute felt in my cock. I've tried to hate her, I've tried to ignore her and act like she's the devil in disguise, but somehow, I can't get her smell from my nose or her smile from my mind. Take away all the other shit that's happened and I can almost see us being happy together. But then I picture her and Michael playing happy families and I want to break some bones.

I've hardly seen Cammie as she's playing the part well as the pissed-off ol' lady. We exchange constant texts and the odd hate fuck, which always ends in an argument about Ava, today being no different. Leaving Rooster on Ava watch, I've spent the last hour inside of Cammie, pretending I'm falling for her.

By the time we re-join them, Cammie has her angry mask on again and it's wearing thin. She sips her drink sourly while glaring at Ava, who's playing some kind of balancing game with Breaker and Taps. They all fall in a heap on the floor, laughter filling the air. It reminds me of old times, when we were all teenagers.

"She's such a whore. How does no one see the flirting and teasing? It's relentless."

I roll my eyes, watching Breaker lay on his back and bench press Ava like she weighs nothing. "She loves the guys like brothers, there's nothing in it."

"Why do you always stick up for her?"

I'm saved from another screaming match when Damien calls me into his office. I rush off gratefully without giving her a response.

"My guy just got back to me. Sit down, you're gonna need this." He places a glass of whisky in my hand.

"News about Cammie?" I ask, and he nods, pacing with the bottle of whisky in his hand.

"Al Monteo," he starts, and I groan.

"Why does that name keep popping back up?" I growl, knocking my drink back.

"Cammie is his sister. Her real name is Camilla Monteo."

I pause, the glass still at my lips. Al's sister? But we were the same age, and Cammie is the same age, which means . . . "Yeah, his twin," confirms Damien as if he read my mind.

"So, what, this is some fucked-up revenge plot?"

Damien shrugs. "I don't know. It makes no sense. Why would she wait this long?"

There's a million questions going through my mind and I stand, heading for the door. "Hey, hey, stop. We can't go out there all guns blazing. We need a plan," says Damien calmly.

"My plan is to get answers doing what I'm best at."

Damien grips my shoulder. "I know you want answers, we all do, but we need to be clever about this. I don't think it's a coincidence that she and Michael are here at the same time. Both want to cause shit, so what if they've teamed up?"

It makes sense as both would hate us and the club. I take a few deep, calming breaths, something I've picked up from my time with Ava. "So, what the fuck do we do now?"

"Let's call church, see what the guys can come up with. Put a prospect on Ava and Evie."

Church is eventful. The guys are pissed when we tell them everything about Ava and Michael and now Cammie. It's hard not to think it's all one big revenge plot. I find myself drifting back to the day we found Ava, her clothes ripped and her face bloody. Her thirteen-year-old body covered in bruises.

Pops stands abruptly, making me flinch. "Cut her fucking throat and watch her bleed out," he yells.

"Pops, I'm with you, but we need to do some digging first. If she's been planted here and doesn't return to whoever sent her, then we're starting a war and we won't even see it coming."

Damien's right but fuck if I'm not agreeing with Pops on this one. "We can make her talk."

"How? You ever tortured a woman Gunner?" snaps Damien.

I sigh. "It can't be that different to a man, they bleed the same."

"No, we need to follow her. You need to dig more, Gunner. Talk to her about the wedding, about her family and if they're coming. Push to meet them, hand-fucking-deliver the invitation if you have to. I'm almost certain that she and Michael are in this together. They both hate us and them turning up around the same time is too much of a coincidence."

There's banging on the door and KP, a prospect, yells, "Pres, we have a situation."

We all head out, rushing into the main room, where Ava is sitting on top of Cammie, punching her over and over. Cammie is trying desperately to claw at Ava's face, and they're both screaming and yelling. I glance around at two prospects, both looking at me for instruction, and I groan. Where the hell are the women when we need them to calm shit down?

"Well, I ain't wading in. Cats got claws," says Rooster, folding his arms.

Cammie manages to throw Ava off her and begins to scramble away, but Ava's been raised by the club and she's soon dragging her back to the ground.

"Jesus Christ," I huff, stomping over and lifting Ava under her arms. She kicks out, catching Cammie on the side of her face. "Stop!" I roar, turning her and throwing her over my shoulder. "Where's the damn kid?"

"I took her to her nan," says KP.

"Gunner, put me down," screams Ava, banging on my back with her tiny fists. I laugh at her attempt to hurt me and march her to the huge boardroom where we hold church. I slam the door and lock it, then sit her on the large oak table and hold her arms by her sides so she can't move.

"What the fuck happened back there?"

"She started on me, calling me a whore. Told me she was gonna fuck my life up like I have hers."

"Did she say what she meant?" I ask, suddenly intrigued by Cammie's confession.

"Who the fuck cares?" she yells.

"I care, Ava. Did she say what she meant?"

Ava takes a few calming breaths before shaking her head. "No, I didn't ask. I assumed she meant because of what happened with us."

Her deep breaths cause her breasts to rise and fall, and my eyes are drawn there, "That was kinda hot, seeing you rolling around like that." I smirk, and she rolls her eyes. "Can you re-do it naked?"

"Yes, if it means I get to punch her again," huffs Ava.

I laugh. No slapping for this little alley cat, Damien and I always told her to punch, giving her self-defence lessons after her attack.

"What am I gonna do with you, Bait?" I sigh, shaking my head.

She looks down at her hands laying in her lap. "I'm sorry for causing all this trouble, Ashton," she says quietly.

The use of my Christian name makes me inhale sharply. It sounds good coming from her lips, and I lean in, nipping at that bottom lip she keeps biting on.

"Life would be boring if you weren't around," I say, licking where I nipped her.

A picture of Michael kissing her suddenly fills my head and I release her arms, taking a step back. "Shit, sorry, I didn't mean . . . just forget it happened. My head's all over." I ignore the rejected look in her eyes, it's not the first time I've seen it, but I can't get past her and Michael. "I have to check on Cammie."

"So, you can forgive her for kissing some biker from the Saints MC but not me for Michael?"

I pause with my back to her, my hand on the door handle. "It isn't the fucking same, Ava," I growl, and then I leave before I say things I'll regret.

Cammie is sitting at the bar, an ice pack to her cheek. She has bruises appearing already, and I wince. "Fuck, baby, it looks bad. Good job we haven't set a date for the wedding yet."

She scowls at me. "Why did you go with her? I was on the goddamn floor and you went with her!"

"She was on top of you, Cam. I got her off and took her away from you. I'm back now, I just had to make sure she was calm before I let her go."

"Whatever happens you're always with her. I'm sick of it."

I take her hand and place gentle kisses on her cheek and neck. "Baby, I told you a million times, you're the one for me. Ava is like a kid sister, an annoying one. You know if she wasn't Damien's sister, I'd have put a bullet in her for some of the shit she's pulled." I kiss her deep, taking my time to taste her mouth. "Let's set a date for the wedding. As soon as possible." I pull back slightly so I can see her reaction, but she doesn't look fazed.

"Yes, good idea. The sooner the better."

"Why don't we drive out to see your parents? I want to do shit properly and speak to your dad," I say, running my hand up and down her back.

"They're really busy, Ashton. Let's just get planning and we'll let them know the details after." She looks up as Ava enters the room. "Tell her. In front of me, tell her you choose me. I'm sick of her looking at you like you belong to her." When I don't speak, she huffs and then leans around me to see Ava as she passes us. "We're setting a date for the wedding. You're not invited!"

Ava looks at Cammie, an annoyed look in her eyes. "And I care because?"

"Because you love him. You love him and you need to stop. Move on and stop going after him. He belongs to me now. He chooses me."

Ava turns her eyes to me, an eyebrow arched, daring me to confirm what Cammie is saying. I have to keep Cammie on side. Damien wants more information, and I won't get that if I blow this. "Don't make this any harder, Ava. Cammie is my ol' lady now, and I have to respect her decisions. You understand that. She's right, you have to move on."

Ava looks fit to burst, her eyes wide as she glares at me. "I have to move on? Me?"

"Ava, enough!"

I sigh with relief at the sound of Damien's voice. Ava turns to him. "What? She started on me."

"Listen to yourself, you sound like a child. Why don't you do us all a favour and fuck off to live with Evie's dad," snaps Cammie.

I exchange a look with Damien, one that says Cammie just fucked up. No one's told her that Evie's dad is back on the scene, and no one's told her that he wants Ava and Evie to move with him.

"And make your life easier? No thanks, I like it here," continues Ava, assuming Cammie knows through me.

"Enough," yells Damien. "Ava, get the fuck out of my face. Gunner, go and make wedding plans. This club needs a good celebration. I'll speak to the vicar and book him for his next available slot. Cammie, get on the phone to your parents. We want to meet them if we're gonna be family."

"You'll meet them on the day, Damien. They're very busy," she says.

"Too busy to have a pre-wedding party for their one and only daughter?" asks Damien.

She shrugs. "Yeah, both are out of town at the moment."

That confirms she's an only child. "Ava, invite Michael, seeing as he's so keen to get back into your bed," I say.

It's a theory I have, but when Cammie glances over to me with shock on her face, I think I may be right. Ava looks outraged, but I give her my best 'shut the fuck up' face. She seems to understand because she closes her mouth and then smiles.

"Not jealous, are you, Gunner? I can't help if your brother can't get enough of me."

Damien looks like he's about to explode, but I shake my head, indicating that it's okay.

"Walking in on you fucking him was exactly like seeing my brother and sister fuck," I snap.

"Michael is with Ava?" asks Cammie quietly, and I nod.

"Disgusting, ain't it? I'll introduce you to him one day, and you'll see what I mean. He's like the cheaper version of me." I kiss her shocked face and then turn to Ava. "Office, now. Damien and I need a new plan of action for your safety."

Once inside the office, I close the door. "That's the connection. Cammie is fucking Michael," I say.

"Really? I can't see that. Who would want to fuck that dirty bitch?" asks Ava before turning to me and smirking. "Oops, sorry, Gunner."

I roll my eyes. "Ava, we know Cammie isn't who she says she is. You were right about her kissing someone else. Damien did some digging."

Ava looks to Damien, and he nods. "You might want to sit down."

She lowers into a chair and then looks between us. "So, who is she?"

"Al Monteo's sister," I say. Ava's eyes go wide, and she begins to hyperventilate, gripping her chest tightly. I crouch in front of her, rubbing her arms gently. "It's okay, Ava," I sooth, waiting until her breathing slows before I continue. "We think she and Michael came back for revenge."

"On who? I didn't do anything wrong," she cries.

"We know, Bait, we know. Maybe they joined forces because they know who killed him," I suggest.

"But they don't know for sure he's dead. According to reports, he just disappeared," says Damien with a frown.

CHAPTER TWELVE

Ava

I take in another deep breath. My heart is pounding so hard, I feel like it might pump out of my aching chest. I have to come clean about the video and trust that these guys can help because I'm out of ideas and options, and they're beginning to connect the dots.

"Michael knows, and if he's in it with Cammie, then she probably knows too." I sigh, and they both look at me, waiting for me to continue. "Michael was there that night. He filmed it."

Damien stands abruptly, causing his office chair to fall backwards. I jump when it crashes to the floor. "What the fuck! How do you know?"

"I've seen it," I mutter.

"Hold on, how long have you known about this?" snaps Gunner, standing and moving away from me. He looks like he wants to hurt me, and I swallow the lump in my throat.

"He first showed it to me when I was nineteen. He used that to blackmail me."

Damien begins pacing, and Gunner turns away from me, placing his hands against the wall and hanging his head. "Fuck," he growls.

"So, what, he blackmailed you into sleeping with him? Why the fuck didn't you come straight to me and tell me everything?" shouts Damien, slamming his hands down on the desk.

"He had something else. At first, I laughed at him, but then he showed me the other video and I just thought it would be easier to do what he wanted rather than hurt everyone. I thought about you and Pops seeing that video and I..." I can't hold it in anymore and I burst in to tears. "He said he would put it all over the internet, send it to all the guys and my friends. He threatened to advertise me on dating sites as a girl who likes to act out rape scenes. He said men would come and attack me thinking I wanted it. And I couldn't..." I take a shaky breath. "I couldn't go through it again."

Gunner crouches back down in front of me and takes my hands. "Jesus, Ava, why the fuck didn't you tell us? We could have ended him."

"Because he said someone else had a copy of the videos, so if he went missing, that person would know what to do with the evidence."

"What was this other video?" asks Damien.

"It's of the night Al Monteo attacked me. He filmed it, and I didn't know."

"Fuck," groans both Damien and Gunner in unison.

"So, how did Michael get that?" asks Damien.

I shrug, it's something I've asked myself over and over. "I don't know."

"We need to get Evie out of here. There're some fake passports for all of us in here," Damien says as he unlocks his safe and searches inside. "I'll have Pops take her and Mum away for a while. Michael won't even know she's gone. Don't answer his calls or arrange to see him."

I nod. I know it's for the best, but sending my baby away is the last thing I want. It breaks my heart.

"Fuck. What a fucking mess. We need to get the guys in and sort this fucker out," says Damien, heading for the door.

Gunner stands staring down at me. He opens his mouth once or twice, then closes it, pressing his lips together. "There's no way out of any of this, Gunner. I've gone over and over it, but he's way too big now. He'll bury this club and no one will bat an eye lid," I say, wiping the tears from my face.

"I want to go there and put a fucking bullet in his head," he growls, placing his hands on the desk in front of him and bowing his head. "What the fuck is his game?"

"I don't think he came back to make me part of this game again. He came back to hurt the club. When he saw Evie, he saw a chance to do that. I'm so fucking stupid, I should have just gone years ago. I'm twenty-four years old and still live here with secrets, hoping they stay hidden. I should have come clean years ago. I was scared to move away from the club in case he made good on his threat and guys turned up at my door," I cry. "I've made it easier for him now, haven't I? I'm gonna lose my daughter."

Gunner stays silent, his back to me. I wish he'd reassure me, but the fact that he doesn't, tells me he's just as worried as me. He knows as well as I do that the only way is to go along with what Michael wants.

He lets out a sound, something between a shout and a growl, that makes me jump, and then I watch as he storms out.

It doesn't take long for Pops to get everything sorted, and I stand at the door hugging Evie to me. I try hard not to cry because I want her to think this is a fun holiday. "I love you. Be really good for Pops and Nan."

She nods, an excited look on her perfect little face. "I love you too, Mummy."

Once they've gone, I go to my room and cry. I feel like there's no end in sight to this mess. I call Chloe. "Can you come over, Chlo? I've told the guys everything, and now I feel it's messier than before." I sigh.

"Of course, I'm on my way."

It takes her fifteen minutes to get to the clubhouse. I'm sitting at the bar waiting for her while the guys are still in church. I guess it'll be a long time before we see any of them. I fill Chloe in on Gunner and Damien's reaction.

"You did the right thing, Ava."

"What if Michael finds out I've told them? It'll take minutes for that video to circulate throughout porn sites. Once it's out there, I can't ever get it back." I let out a sob, and she comforts me, reassuring me that we'll work it out.

Gunner

We've been in church for almost an hour and we still have fuck all. Every situation ends up with someone either going inside or the video of Ava's rape being sent out to every fucking perverted bastard out there. The thought of her thirteen-year-old self being shared on the internet for people's pleasure makes me sick. I knock another whisky back to ease it.

"Man, we got nothing. He's too well known for us to just remove him," says Tap.

An idea begins to form and I stand, making everyone's eyes turn to me. "That's what we do," I say. "We take him, hold him. How long will it take for that pussy to cave and beg for mercy? He'll give us the footage."

"And then what? We just set him free, let him go off into the sunset?" asks Damien. "Then what will happen? You don't think he'll bring us down? He's got power now, Gunner, he'll take us out."

"How about we keep Cammie? Maybe we can get it out of her who she's working with, what they want, what they have, and where they have it?" Maddocks suggests.

Damien rubs his chin in thought. "But what if whoever she works for misses her and reports it to the police, this is the first place Michael will come looking."

"I'll tell her we're going away to celebrate the engagement. She'll tell Michael she'll be out of touch, by which time we may have a plan," I say.

"That'll work." Damien nods. "Okay, let's go with that, cos we have fuck all else. Set the plan in action, Gunner. Let's hope we're right and she squeals."

Maddocks stands and grins as he heads out. "I'll sharpen my toolkit."

Maddocks is the best man for the job. Being the Enforcer, he has ways of making people talk. We haven't had to be brutal in a long time.

I find Cammie in my room. She looks up from her phone, still pouting. I dive onto the bed next to her and nip at her exposed thigh.

"Baby, I've been thinking," I smile, "I want to take you away to make up for all the shit that's gone down lately. Ava has been bringing all kinds of drama to the club. Let's get away from it all. We can make wedding plans and work on your tan for the big day."

She ponders this for a minute and then smiles. "Okay, when?"

I get out my phone. "I'll book us something as soon as. Maybe there are flights for tomorrow, if that's not too short notice?"

She shakes her head and jumps off the bed. "You book, I'll pop home and pack. I'll be back soon." She kisses me on the head and bounces out the room. I shove the phone back in my pocket and groan into the quilt. How the fuck did I fall for her? I thought she got me, that she was the one, and all along, she's been plotting with my half-brother.

By the time Cammie comes back, my mood has taken a darker turn. I haven't told Damien that I've already put the plan in place, so I drop him a text telling him to get ready, that I'll be bringing her to him in the next half-hour.

Cammie stands her suitcase next to my stool at the bar. I take a gulp of my beer without looking in her direction. "Did you book anywhere?" She smiles, kissing my cheek.

"Oh yeah, baby, you're gonna remember this break for some time."

Cammie gives an excited squeal. "Oh my god, where?"

"It's a surprise," I say, my eyes catching Ava as she enters the room with Chloe. She looks lighter somehow, like maybe she's unloaded to Chloe. I admire her long tanned legs, her short shorts only just covering her arse cheeks. She laughs at something Chloe says, and my lip lifts slightly. It's good to see her smile. Cammie catches the movement and then follows my gaze to Ava.

"Really? You're still gonna watch her while I stand in front of you?"

I nod once, then bring my eyes to Cammie's outraged face. "I've loved Ava since she was a kid, and not just like a sister. She's had some real bad shit happen to her, and look at her, she's still smiling. I fucking love her. I always have."

Cammie's eyes almost hit her forehead in surprise. "Are you drunk?"

I shake my head. "I learnt something today. Ava has always had my back. I didn't realise it, and I hate myself for that, because she's carried on protecting me even though I've been a real bastard to her."

"I don't understand, what the hell are you saying?"

She plays a good game, I'll give her that. If I didn't know the truth, I'd almost believe she was heartbroken. Her hand rears back to slap me, but I expect it, so as she brings it back, I catch it in my hand and grip her wrist tight. "Don't even think about it, Cameron. Or should I call you Camilla?" I ask, tipping my head to one side in thought.

Her face freezes and her anger is replaced by fear. I rip her shirt in one swift movement, checking she isn't bugged. There's no visible wire, but I pull out the handheld scanner that Grill gave me. Once I'm satisfied she isn't bugged, I spin her around so she's facing away from me and pull her arms behind her back. She lets out a shout, and

I press my mouth to her ear. "Camilla Monteo, nice to meet you," I whisper, then I reach into her back pocket and take out her mobile phone, chucking it on the bar.

"You have no idea what you're bringing to this club if you don't let me out of here," she screeches, thrashing about.

Ava and Chloe approach. "What's going on?" asks Chloe.

"Feeling a bit kinky." I wink, and Cammie huffs, pulling at her wrists to try and loosen my grip.

"Does Damien know?" asks Ava.

I laugh. "What, that I'm kinky? No, Bait."

Tap hands me some rope, and I bind her wrists behind her back. I use her thumb to open her mobile and sit her on the bar stool next to me. I smile, and she glowers at me. "Make yourselves scarce," I say to Chloe and Ava.

Once they've left, I flick through Cammie's phone. There's nothing much, hardly any texts except ones to me, so I assume she's been clever enough to delete any evidence.

I hear the thud of Damien's boots as he comes up from the cellar. "Ah, she's back, good timing."

I tuck her phone into my back pocket and stand, pulling her to her feet also. "This is ridiculous. You won't get away with it," she screams as I pull her towards the stairs that lead down to the cellar.

As we descend, the damp smell fills my nostrils. I don't remember the last time I came down here, since we don't use it that often these days. Once we get to the bottom, I drag her across the dark, dank room until we reach an old shelf unit. Damien pushes in on one side to reveal a door. After he knocks on it twice, the door swings open and the creak echoes through the room.

Cammie begins to struggle, pushing back against me. Maybe she's only just realised how serious this shit is about to get. "Gunner, please, we can sort it," she begs.

I grin at Damien, knowing she'll crack easily. I lift her up around the waist and carry her through the doorway. Her struggling is annoying me.

We walk along a narrow tunnel. It was dug out years ago, maybe even before Pops started the club, and it leads us to a small room that we call The Den. There's a metal bed in the corner that reminds me of something that would have been used in a mental institute years back. The mattress is thin and covered in plastic, and there're wrist restraints secured to the wall on chains.

In the middle of the room is a metal chair, and above it is one single light bulb that flickers. It leaves the room dimly lit, and it takes a minute for my eyes to adjust.

Maddocks stands in one corner, a mad glint in his eye. He's holding the bag that contains his tools. I'm hoping it doesn't get that far, not because I give a shit about Cammie but because I hate hearing women scream in pain. It goes against everything I believe in.

I force her down onto the chair and cut the rope from her wrists. She rubs at them briefly before Damien reaches down to the side of the chair and pulls up a set of handcuffs which he places on her wrists.

"So, Camilla, this is how it's gonna work. I'm gonna ask you a question, and you're gonna answer. If you don't, things are going to get very messy. Are we clear?" asks Damien, taking a step back from her. When she doesn't answer, he continues. "What are you doing in our club?"

"You killed my brother," she spits out angrily.

"I don't know what you're talking about. Your brother went missing as far as I know."

"I'm not stupid. You killed him for her," she snaps, "because of what she said he did to her."

"You mean when he raped my thirteen-year-old sister?" Damien grates out.

"He didn't rape her, she wanted it. Have you seen how she is? With your own men under your nose, that's how she was with my brother."

Damien shakes his head and then hits Cammie across the face, her head falling to the side. "He groomed my fucking teenage sister on the internet so he could carry out his sick fantasies with his friends. So, don't sit in front of me telling me that she asked for it. She was just a kid!"

"You're all so blind to her." Cammie begins to laugh. "And now, you're all going to die to protect her."

"Nobody's dying in my club. How long have you been fucking Michael?" snaps Damien.

She presses her lips together. "I don't know who Michael is."

It's my turn to laugh, and she looks to me. "Come on, sweetheart, you're crap at lying."

"I lied to you for long enough. Do you know how hard it was sucking your dick all this time? It makes my skin crawl just thinking about it," she spits out.

"You're shit at lying and you loved sucking my dick. Wonder what your brother would have thought about that." I grin.

"My brother's dead. You bastards killed him," she yells, tugging harder to get herself free.

"We didn't kill your brother. What's Michael's part in all this?" asks Damien.

"As if I'm going to tell you anything," she shouts.

Damien nods to Maddocks, who steps forward and places his bag on the floor. He opens it slowly and pulls out various items, laying them on the floor in a neat line.

"Well, you'd better tell us something or Maddocks here is gonna start making a mess," says Damien, sighing.

She grins. "You'll find out soon enough."

I grip her hair and pull her head back so she's looking up at me. "There's nothing left now. You ain't walking out of here, and we're going for Michael. Make a start, Maddocks, we'll come back later," I snarl, storming from the room with Damien on my heels.

He sighs. "I thought she'd spill."

I wince as a scream follows us through the tunnel. "It won't take long."

I'm wrong. It's been eight hours since we took her to The Den. She hasn't talked, and I'm getting more annoyed by the second. As I get closer to the dark, dingy room, I can smell a mix of dampness, piss, and blood. I screw my nose up as I enter and the smell almost chokes me. Cammie is on the bed, her arms above her head, chained to the wall. Her shirt is still open where I ripped it to check for a wire. She must be freezing, as it's cold down here.

She looks at me, squinting in the poor lighting. I take a seat on the metal chair. "Make it easier on yourself, Cammie." I sigh, putting my head in my hands.

I'm surprised when she begins to cry, her soft sobs filling the air. "Tell me the truth. If I'm not getting out of here, then tell me, did you kill Al?"

I take a deep breath, remembering that night like it was yesterday, and then I nod. She isn't leaving here alive, so she deserves to go to her grave knowing the truth. It's the least I can do to give her some peace. "Yes, I put a bullet in him after we beat him half to death. He was the first person I killed. I don't regret it."

She sobs a little harder but nods. She almost looks grateful for the truth. "What did you do with him? Where did you put him after?"

"He was burnt, at a crematorium."

"Good. I don't like the thought of him being buried, not alone."

I sigh. "Cam, what was the plan? What were you gonna do to us, to me?"

"It wasn't my idea. I wanted you to pay for Al, but I wasn't going to do anything myself. I hooked up with a guy from another MC. He knew Michael and introduced us. Michael knew all about me and Al, and he offered me revenge for Al if I got in with you to feed information back to him. He was pissed when I couldn't offer anything cos you never told me stuff. I don't know what his original plan was. I think he wanted to bust you for shit, but then he found out about Ava having Evie and his plans changed. He wants to get them both and then he's going to bust you for Al's murder."

I steeple my fingers to my mouth, running my forefinger back and forth across my bottom lip. "Where does he keep the evidence?"

"He has it on a memory stick. It's in his office. I have the other copy in my bag, and that's it apart from the copy on his phone," she mutters. "I've told you everything, Gunner. Let me go. I won't tell him, I promise."

I move towards her and pull her up to sit. I hold her against me and kiss the side of her head. I'll be sorry about this death, more than any other, but she fucked with the club, and I'm not convinced she won't come back, especially now she knows the truth. She pulls back, confused, and then her eyes widen in shock as I push the knife into her heart. She makes a choked gurgling sound and convulses a few times before going still in my arms. I lay her back on the bed and close her eyes.

I sit for a while. The peace is a welcome break from the constant noise of the clubhouse. My heart aches because, despite everything, I felt something for Cam. Her betrayal has left a mark, and I berate myself for the hundredth time for falling for her lies. I should have seen her for what she was.

I make my way back up to the clubhouse, careful to lock the door and pull the shelf unit back into place. The clubhouse is quiet, and the only sound in the main room is the buzzing of the fridges behind the bar. Usually, there are still bikers hanging around, but I think all the news about Ava has taken its toll on everyone.

As I approach my room, Ava stumbles from hers and crashes into my chest. She squeaks and looks up at me, surprise on her face. "Sorry, I didn't expect anyone to be wandering about," she whispers. I stare down at her for an uncomfortable length of time. She gives a nervous smile and then goes to move past me, but I snatch her wrist up in my hand, halting her steps.

"What's wrong, Gunner?" she asks, her beautiful blue eyes staring up at me.

I slowly lower my head, and she takes in a deep, shaky breath. "I fucked up. You had my back, and I fucked up. I'm sorry for that," I whisper.

Ava shrugs and then I place a soft kiss against the side of her mouth. "Gunner..."

I don't give her chance to protest. Instead, I press my mouth against hers in a deep, hungry kiss. Our tongues clash, and I find myself pushing her back into her room, but then I pull away, gripping her shoulders in my large hands. Our breathing mingles together as we try to gain control. "I wasted so much time," I mutter, more to myself than her, but she nods in understanding.

I reach for the buttons on her night shirt, slowly and carefully unfastening each one, keeping eye contact with her as I work down the shirt. Once it falls open, I realise she's naked underneath, and her pink nipples pucker against the cold. I lean down, and she places her small hands against my hard chest as I flick my hot tongue over the pointy tip. She hisses and digs her fingers into my skin. I move to the other, taking it into my mouth and gently sucking. It drives her crazy, and she lets out soft moans as I continue the slow torture. I gently push her to sit on the edge of her bed, and then I guide her to lay back. Peppering kisses along her shoulder blade, I lean my weight on my hands at either side of her head. I work the kisses downwards, along her chest, across her stomach. and along her legs. Kneeling, I place kisses carefully along her inner thighs.

I run kisses back up as she squirms against me, trying to guide my mouth to the spot she wants me most. I smile to myself, lightly blowing against her opening. I lean in and press my tongue against her swollen clit. She groans, and I lick, careful to press on her clit with each swipe of my tongue. I insert my finger into her pussy, liking the way she shivers. She's close, and I increase the pace, moving faster, nipping and licking harder until she presses her thighs against my head, screaming out as she orgasms against my mouth. Ava goes floppy, her breaths heavy. I make my way up her body, taking my hard shaft in my hand and pressing against her opening.

It feels too good to take it slow, but I control myself. I want this to feel different, not just because I owe her everything, but because I want her to feel how I feel. Finally, I *need* her to feel how I feel.

I brace myself on my hands again as I push in inch by inch. I stop, taking a few breaths to ease the urge to ram into her and fuck her hard. Her eyes are fixed on me, the blue in them appearing darker than normal. Her cheeks are flushed, and her lips make that cute 'o' shape that she does. I grip her hands in mine, holding them above her head, then I begin to move slowly, back and forth, taking my time, enjoying each thrust that causes her to groan.

As the pleasure begins to build, my movements become jerky. I run my tongue along her bottom lip, biting on it gently and tugging. A familiar warmth spreads throughout my body and I thrust faster, moving a hand to grip her leg, pushing it to bend at the knee, getting a deeper angle. Ava begins to shake, grasping the sheets above her head and letting out an unsteady cry. I feel her pussy gripping me hard, and it sends me over the edge. I release into her on a shout, holding the last thrust deep inside her as I spill into her.

We lay, staring at each other as our breathing slow again. "That was unexpected," she finally says.

I lean down and kiss her. "It should have happened a long time ago."

I stand, taking her by the hands and pulling her up. Throwing back her quilt, I climb into bed and tug her with me. She lays with her back against me, and I shuffle her until she's pressed so tight against me, I can feel my cock getting hard again.

CHAPTER THIRTEEN

Ava

I'm too hot. I try to get free, but there's too much pressure. I begin to thrash about, panicking, and then I hear a voice. It's distant, but I recognise it. "Ava, it's okay. Ava . . ."

My eyes open, and I sit up, gasping for breath. Gunner is in front of me, his expression worried. I grip my chest, looking around in panic. "I'm here. You're okay, Bait," he says quietly, gently stroking my arm.

"Sorry, did I wake you?"

He smiles, taking my hand and kissing it. "Don't worry. It's later than I normally sleep."

There's a banging on the door, making me jump. "Are you in there, Gunner?" It's Damien, and he doesn't sound happy.

Gunner sighs and gets off the bed, pulling a sheet around his naked waist. He opens the door, stepping back and allowing Damien to stomp in. "Did you do it?" he demands.

Gunner gives a nod. "I got what we needed. She talked."

"And now she's fucking dead, what the hell am I supposed to do with her? I can't move her yet and she'll stink the place out," he yells.

"I'll meet you in ten in the office. I need to speak to you and Ava about what we do next," says Gunner.

Ten minutes later, I sit in the chair opposite my brother. Gunner chooses to stand. "This is copy one," he says, holding up a memory stick. "Cammie had it in her bag."

"And copy two is?" asks Damien.

"In a safe in Michael's office, and he also has one on his mobile phone."

"Great, how the hell do we break into the office of the chief of police?" Damien growls.

Gunner sighs. "We don't. I have a plan, but neither of you will like it."

I sit up in the chair, waiting for his plan. Damien takes the memory stick from Gunner and plugs it into his computer. I dive up, but he waves his hand at me to stop.

"You can't watch that," I screech.

"I don't plan to. Gunner is, just to check it's what she says it is."

Gunner groans and then pulls the laptop towards him. He skims through the first video and then watches two seconds of the next one before pausing it. "Yep, that's the one," he huffs, not looking pleased at all.

I cover my burning face with my hands, but Gunner crouches in front of me, pulling them away. "Don't be embarrassed, baby. What happened was out of your hands." He kisses me softly on the lips before standing again.

"So, what, you kill your ex and move on to my sister?" snaps Damien.

"You killed Cammie?" I ask, and Gunner nods, not looking overly happy about it either.

"The plan is," he says, ignoring my brother, "I lay low, like I'm still away with Cammie. Ava, you'll need to get real good at acting."

I groan because this does not sound like a good plan. "Why?"

"Because you'll have to tell him you want to move into his condo."

Damien stands at the same time I protest in anger. "No chance. Anyway, he wants Evie too."

"Then you make up some shit about her being on a pre-planned holiday. Sell it to him, something about spending time just you two, so you can get to know one another properly."

"And if he doesn't fall for it?"

"He will. He wants to take you from me and Damien. Once he's a bit more trusting, you'll turn up to his office, dressed up to fuck his brains out. You're gonna get all kinky, tie him up, blindfold him. Then, you're gonna let us in, and we're gonna break that safe and take his shit."

"That won't ever work. He'll hear you, for a start, and you're gonna be there while I get my freak on with him?"

"No way. I'll bring a club girl to suck his cock while we get the job done. Maddocks will have some gear to open the safe, and we'll be in and out."

"But in the meantime, I've got to seduce him. I hate his guts, he knows I do. He'll never fall for it."

"It's the only plan I've got, Bait. It's got to work. Those offices will be monitored and there will be police around twenty-four-seven. I know him, he'll be at his desk all the time working on his plan to crush us. We have to distract him."

"And how will you get in there with police everywhere?" I ask.

"I can get us some police uniforms." He grins, and I roll my eyes and turn to Damien, who looks pleased.

"So, you're happy with this plan?" I groan, and he nods.

"It makes sense," says Damien. "And we have nothing else."

We go over the plan, throwing in different ideas and making improvements. Eventually, I pull out my phone and send a text under Damien's watchful eye.

Me: Can we meet to talk?
Michael: My place in an hour.

He follows that with an address.

An hour later, I stand nervously in front of an apartment door. It's in a nice part of town, with a security desk in the foyer. I had to show ID before they'd even buzz his apartment.

The door opens and Michael stands there looking smug. "What brings you here, princess?"

"I've had an argument with Damien. Gunner is away with his whore, and Damien decided to take it upon himself to send our daughter away on holiday without telling me."

His face turns red and he drags me into the apartment, slamming the door. "So, what made you think you could come here?"

"Well, I guess I thought it would be a chance for us to talk," I say, looking around the large living area. It's clear he has a cleaner because the place is almost clinical, with nothing out of place and not one spec of dust on any surface. It reeks of money.

"Talk about what?" He indicates for me to go and take a seat on the sofa, which I do, trying to stop my hands from shaking.

"Well, I know we need to wait for the results, but I also know Evie is yours, so I wanted to talk a bit more about your offer." He frowns, sitting down next to me. "To live nearby you," I add, just to clarify.

"I own the apartment downstairs. It's similar to this one but a bit smaller. So, you're willing to leave The Eagles and move in here?" He smirks.

"What choice do I have? I love my daughter, and I know you'll take her away from me if I don't agree."

"And have you told your big brother about your plans?"

I shake my head. "I'm just going to leave and then tell him. I don't want him to cause a scene, and he won't understand my reasons."

He runs his finger along my bare thigh. I wore the denim shorts because I knew it would distract him. "He'll hate it. So will Ashton."

I nod in agreement. "Well, they have to stop controlling me someday."

"You're making the right decision." He grins, leaning in towards me. I lean back, trying to avoid his lips on mine, but this spurs him on and, somehow, I end up lying flat with him resting on top of me. He likes the fight, and if I just gave in, he'd be suspicious, so I wriggle under him, trying to throw him off. He wraps a fist in my hair and holds me in place so he can kiss me.

"When will my daughter be back?" he asks.

"Soon. Maybe I can move in sooner, get settled and ready for when she comes back?"

He smiles and nods. "Good thinking. I'll get the cleaners to give it a once-over."

Michael gets off me, and I stand. "Call me."

As soon as I get out into the fresh air, I wipe at my face, disgust making me shiver against the warm summer breeze. How the hell will I keep him off me? I walk around the corner and get into the waiting car.

"Done?" asks Gunner, gripping the steering wheel tight. He insisted on driving me here, mainly because he thought it would give me peace of mind, but secretly, I think he wanted to make sure I was in and out. I don't know what he planned to do if I was longer than the agreed ten minutes.

"Yeah," I mutter.

"Did he try anything?"

I avoid his stony glare. "He kissed me."

His grip on the steering wheel turns his knuckles white. "We can't wait until you move in. You're gonna have to turn up at his office sooner. We can't risk him forcing you again."

I nod in agreement. The last thing I want is to be used as Michael's plaything. I'd rather get the job done sooner.

When we return to the clubhouse, Gunner calls church to discuss bringing the plan forward. I mooch around the club, cleaning and keeping busy. I miss Evie already and part of me wishes I was back at work just so I was busy. Instead, I keep going over things in my head, wondering what will happen to us all if the plan goes wrong, then everything I've done for the last few years will be for nothing.

My phone vibrates indicating a text message. It's Michael telling me how happy he is that I've made the right choice and that he will have the apartment ready by tomorrow. I reply with a thumbs up emoji. He messages back telling me to think of ways to say thank you to him, and I give a shudder. *What a creep.*

Chloe breezes in looking happy in a little yellow summer dress and shades. She takes one look at the cleaning product and cloth in my hand and whips her shades off. "Oh dear, what's happened?" She takes my arm and guides me to a seat at the bar, and I fill her in on the plan.

"I told you they'd find a way to help," she says.

"You seem very happy today," I say suspiciously, and she grins wider, picking imaginary fluff from her cotton dress.

"Well, maybe I have a reason to smile."

"Please give me something to smile about," I beg, and she laughs.

"I met someone," she says excitedly. "He's amazing and . . ." She trials off when Damien appears behind her, his face cold and unamused.

"Don't let me stop you," he snaps.

"And I really like him," she says quietly, all excitement gone.

I smile. "That's great news, Chloe. I'm so pleased for you. Tell me all about him."

I'm glad she's found someone. Damien had his chance, and now, he needs to realise Chloe won't wait around forever. He stomps around behind the bar, moving bottles and crates. It's a job he doesn't ever do, so I know he's sticking around to hear what Chloe has to say.

"He works at the gym. He's twenty-seven and really fit. A body to die for, and he's so nice to me."

Damien snorts, and Chloe and I exchange an eye roll. "I can't wait to meet him," I say.

"He's meeting my parents next weekend. They're both in town, so thought I'd better schedule something because who knows when they'll next be back."

Damien slams a crate on the floor and the bottles rattle. "Hold on a minute. You're taking him to meet your parents? How long have you known him?"

"Not long, but that doesn't matter. When you know, you know," she says, a cocky glint in her eye.

"Oh please, you said the same about that pool boy," he huffs.

"He was a lifeguard, Damien, and I liked him, but this feels different."

"Yeah, whatever. I give it a month before he cheats on you and you're back here crying and eating me out of ice cream."

She grins. "In a month, I'll be on holiday with him. We just booked the Canary Islands for a week."

Damien looks fit to burst. He rubs at his forehead in frustration, and I try hard to hide my smile. "You booked a holiday? What if he's a nut job? What if he kills you out there?"

"What if he doesn't? What if he's the one I'm supposed to marry and have babies with?" she asks dreamily.

"Fuck's sake, Chloe, fairy tales don't exist."

"Hey," I say in her defence, "if she's happy, leave her." He huffs again and then stomps off. "Think he may be a tad jealous." I smile, and she shrugs.

"He had his chance. I'm moving on."

"Talking of chances," I say slowly, "Gunner and I spent the night together."

Chloe's eyes widen. "What the hell?"

"I know. It was different this time, though. It wasn't a fuck. He took his time, and then afterwards, he stayed. It was nice."

"Just stay guarded, Ava," she says softly. "He doesn't deserve you."

Chloe's right. I've been here before with Gunner, and doubt begins to fill my mind. What if it was because he felt guilty once he knew what I'd sacrificed for him, for this club? "I will. I know it's probably nothing serious. Maybe he just needed someone after Cammie and all that."

Gunner joins us. He looks angry, but he kisses me on the head and then goes behind the bar and gets himself a beer. "What are you two plotting?"

Chloe and I exchange a look. "I'm wondering what your intentions are with my best friend," says Chloe bluntly.

I feel my face turn red with embarrassment as Gunner turns to look at me. "That's none of your business, Chloe," he says.

"It is if I'm the one picking up the pieces," she tells him.

"Right now, I've got a lot of shit on my plate. When I get that sorted, I'll be sure to fill Ava in on my intentions. Until then, you stay the fuck outta my business."

We stare after him as he storms back towards Damien's office. "Jesus, Chlo, what is it with you and putting labels on everything? That was so embarrassing," I whisper.

"Well, I want him to know I'm watching," she says.

"I'm sure he's worried about that," I mutter sarcastically, shaking my head.

Once Chloe leaves, I head to my room. I'm surprised to find Gunner laying on my bed on his stomach, his face towards the door, fast asleep. I smile. I like him being in my bed, waiting for me. I undress, pull on his T-shirt, and then climb into bed next to him. He stirs and wraps his strong arm around me, pulling me to him and throwing a leg over me. I lay awake for some time, trying not to see too much into the fact that he's here with me again. This is the most time we've spent together.

My phone beeps with a text message, and I reach over to grab my phone and open it.

Michael: What are you doing right now? I'm stuck at the office catching up on paperwork. Take my mind off it!

A plan hatches—this could be the perfect opportunity. It's ten in the evening, so I'm sure his office will be quiet. I nudge Gunner, and he stirs, groaning. "Gunner, wake up," I whisper.

He moves against me, his erection pressing against my thigh. "What's up, Bait?"

"Michael's at the office. This could be the perfect time."

Gunner opens his eyes. "Now?"

I nod. "Can you get the guys together? It's only ten o'clock."

He nods and sits up, suddenly wide awake as he reaches for his phone.

Me: I'm drunk, alone at the bar. Why don't I come and say that thank you now? Keep you busy for a while?

His reply comes almost immediately.

Michael: What are you waiting for?

I get up and head for my wardrobe. Searching through, I pull out a short red dress. It screams slutty and has been at the back of my wardrobe for years. I pull it on under Gunner's annoyed but watchful eye. "Don't fuck him," he mutters.

"Then get the shit you need quick," I say, rushing to add a small amount of makeup. "I've told him I'm drunk, otherwise, he wouldn't fall for me going there. He knows I hate him. Pass me your bottle." I point to Gunner's whisky on the floor at the side of my bed. He hands it to me, and I down a few mouthfuls, wincing as it burns my throat.

"Don't actually get drunk," he snaps. "You need to think clearly."

I roll my eyes. "I just need to smell of it," I say.

We stop the car just around the corner from Michael's office. There're a few lights on, but it doesn't look busy. I turn back to Gunner. He looks ridiculous in a police uniform, and I laugh again. "Focus," he snaps. "Get in there, flirt and tie him up, then text me the minute he's secure."

I nod, kissing him on the lips, and then I get out of the car. I sway a little as I make my way to the office just in case he happens to be watching out the window. I keep my head down, my hair covering my face as I approach the entrance. There are buttons by the door, so I buzz the one that says 'Mr. Gunn's Secretary'. Michael's voice crackles through the intercom.

"It's me," I say.

The door buzzes and clicks open. I head for the elevator and press number two for Michael's floor. The doors open and I'm relieved to see there's no one on this floor. Michael's in an office at the back of the room, and full glass windows display him sitting at his desk staring at me. I do my best to sway and stumble as I make my way to him.

He grins. "Someone's had one too many."

I make my way around his desk, giggling. I stumble and fall towards him, placing my hands on his chest.

"I've come to say thank you." I grin, kissing him. Straddling his lap, my skirt rides up my thighs as I kiss him hungrily. I picture Gunner in my head and rock myself back and forth against him.

"Fuck, Ava, I've never seen you like this," Michael pants.

Damn right, he hasn't. Every time this man has been near me, it's been against my will. I rip his shirt open, and he gasps. I rake my nails down his chest lightly and then lick up his neck.

"Whisky makes me crazy." I grin, loosening his tie. "And kinky," I add, giggling.

He winks. "I'll buy you a cupboard full."

"Have you got handcuffs?" I whisper, and he smiles.

"In the top left drawer."

I lean over to reach for the drawer and then cringe because he sees it as the perfect opportunity to run his hand up my inner thigh. He rubs a thumb over my clit as I find the cuffs and hold them up in the air like I've won a victory. I can't wait to get his hands off of me.

I attach one end of the cuffs to his wrist and the other to the arm rest on his chair. I get his tie and wrap it around the other wrist, securing that one to the other arm rest on the chair.

I rock against him, rubbing against his erection, and I groan for added effect. I open my bag and pull out a satin scarf. "Do you like being tied up, Michael?" I ask in what I hope is a seductive voice as I run the scarf across his bare chest. I lean in and run my tongue across his nipple.

"I've never been tied up," he says. "You know I like it rough, Ava."

I hold the scarf to his eyes and tie it around the back of his head. "You're in for a treat then," I whisper close to his ear. I stand, and he stills.

"Where are you?"

I run my finger down his chest. "Right here, officer." I lean across his desk and quietly pick up the intercom, flicking the unlock button and leaving it off the hook so it doesn't lock.

I press my arse against Michael's erection and rub while I grab my phone and send a text to Gunner telling him to come up. I reach for Michael's belt and slowly unbuckle it, then I undo the fastening on his trousers and begin to lower them. He lifts so I can get them down, and a minute later, Hayley appears, barefoot. She usually works at The Eagles' strip club, but Damien offered triple wages tonight for this instead. She gives me a wink and then takes my place in front of Michael.

She pulls at his boxers and frees his erection, running her hand up and down it. Michael throws his head back. "Fuck, baby, that's good. I love this playful side of you."

"Yeah?" I smile, and he nods.

Hayley licks around his tip, and he growls, pulling at his restraints. "I need to fuck you," he groans.

I wait for Hayley to stop before replying, "It's my thank you to you, so it has to be my way."

Hayley proceeds to suck him, and I give a nod to the guys who are all waiting to enter. Maddocks quietly sets about attaching wires to the door of the safe and then attaches them to some kind of handheld computer device.

Gunner looks pissed, glancing at me and then Hayley, who's doing a great job of giving head. "I'm gonna tie you up and fuck your arse. Let me out of these, Ava," growls Michael. Gunner's face goes red with anger. "I want you to struggle. I want to hear you scream," he carries on.

I squeeze Gunner's hand in reassurance, but he pulls away, focussing back on Maddocks. A few clicks and a well-timed groan from Hayley and then Maddocks is in the safe. He shines a torch inside and then holds up several memory sticks with a grin.

Gunner takes them and shoves them into his pocket. Maddocks quietly closes the safe and stands. He mimes the word 'phone', and I realise that I still need Michael's phone.

I find it on the desk and hand it over to him. Gunner taps Hayley on the shoulder, and she pulls away from Michael. "Don't stop, baby, I was almost there," moans Michael.

"Sorry, I have a better surprise," I smile, loosening the blindfold. It falls from his eyes and he blinks a few times to adjust his eyes back to the room. He looks around from me to Hayley and then the guys. It dawns on him that he's been played somehow, and his eyes fall to the safe.

"Too late," says Gunner, holding up the memory sticks.

Michael lets out a nervous laugh. "I told you what would happen, Ava."

"Don't fucking speak to her," Gunner growls, pulling me to his side. "Your threats won't work anymore. We have the videos. It's over, Michael."

"You don't think I have the only copy, do you? The other person is under instruction that if anything happens to me, they're to post that video everywhere. You'll be inside, so who will protect the princess then?"

Gunner smiles. "You mean the copy that I got from Camilla Monteo?"

Michael's face freezes. "We had quite a conversation with Cammie," adds Maddocks.

"She couldn't wait to tell us your plans," Gunner says, throwing an arm around my shoulders. "She gave up the copy quite easily, right before I sent her off to see her brother."

Understanding dawns across Michael's face and then he begins to struggle, pulling hard on the restraints that hold him in place.

"You can't do anything to me. I am the chief of—"

"Blah fucking blah. Don't shit yourself, Michael, we aren't gonna kill you. We ain't that kind of club," says Maddocks.

Hayley begins to undress as Michael looks around panicked. I turn as Damien enters the room. He's in casual clothes, his kutte the only thing missing. Hayley straddles Michael, gripping his shoulders and throwing her head back, looking like she's mid-passion. Maddocks snaps various photos.

Damien perches on the edge of Michael's desk. "So, Michael, here we are." He sighs. "I'm not sure if I ever apologised to you on behalf of

The Eagles Motorcycle Club for everything that happened to you and your mum." Hayley steps away from Michael as he growls and tugs again at his restraints.

"Now, don't get upset, I just want to say that in light of everything that went down with your mum, this club is against drugs. We make sure this town is clear of anything that isn't supplied by us. That way, we know what comes in and what goes out. Everything is clean cut and there's less crime with us controlling the area. I think you'll agree that we actually help this town."

"You're fucking criminals and it's my job to get rid of you," growls Michael.

"Ouch," says Gunner with an amused grin, shaking his head. "Now, now, Michael, be nice."

"We're going to come to an agreement, Michael. You stay away from our club, from my sister, and from her daughter. If you don't, we'll be back, and next time, we won't let you live," Damien says firmly. "Maddocks here has some very naughty photos of you and the gorgeous Hayley. They might find themselves on posters all over town. Hayley's husband is an undertaker and he helps the club out lots. You really don't want him to see these pictures."

"And who knows what we'll find on all these," adds Gunner, holding up the memory sticks with a smile. "But I'm guessing your hold on a lot of people will now be over."

"You're all scum," yells Michael, pulling hard at the restraints.

"You brought this on yourself, thinking you could rape Ava over and over, using a video to blackmail her," shouts Gunner.

Michael laughs. "She loves it, hard and rough, and that's exactly how she takes it, Ashton. I've had her pussy dripping over me."

I squeeze Gunner's hand, and he takes a calming breath. "I should kill you, but none of it matters now, cos I won, Michael. In the end, I won."

"You call her winning?" Michael laughs. "Keep her. Men will always use her because she reeks of weakness. You'll spend the rest of your life protecting her because she attracts trouble."

"Just keep away from her and Evie," orders Damien.

"I don't want the whore or her brat. I got the test rushed through, and it isn't even mine."

The words hit my brain a second after Gunner's and his hand drops from mine. "Fuck this bullshit, we're out of here," he growls, storming from the office.

CHAPTER FOURTEEN

Gunner

I get in the car, grip the steering wheel, and take a few deep breaths. Blood is rushing through me and pounding in my ears. Ava fucking lied. The kid isn't Michael's, which means there's someone else out there, someone else who could pop up at any time and break us apart. I bang my hands against the steering wheel and let out a string of curse words.

The passenger door opens and the car springs groan in protest as Maddocks gets in. "Thought Ava could get a lift back with Damien. Didn't think you'd want to sit with her right now."

"I just started to think we can work, Mad, then something else comes up. Michael's right—Ava attracts trouble."

"Come on, man, that's not fair. She's spent years protecting you and Damien, at least hear her out."

"Why, so she can tell me another sob story of how it's not her fault? Fuck that."

"That's harsh. Rein it the fuck in before we get back to the clubhouse," Maddocks snaps, glaring at me.

I watch angrily as Damien leads Ava and Hayley from the building. Ava tries to catch my eye, but I look away and start the engine. I'm too pissed to talk to her right now.

"I'd love to be a fly on the wall in the morning. We left the fucker with his pants round his ankles and his limp dick hanging out." Maddocks laughs, trying to lift the mood. It doesn't work—all I can think about is Ava.

We get back to the clubhouse, and I follow Maddocks straight to his room. We want to check the memory sticks to find out just how many people Michael's been blackmailing.

We spend hours going through footage. Some of it is too unclear to make out. We find Ava's and the video linking me and Damien to Al Monteo's murder. Maddocks pockets that to give to Ava, saying she should destroy it so she knows it's gone.

"Now, we're talking." Maddocks grins, pausing the video. I get up from the bed where I was checking my mobile and lean over his shoulder. "This is the top dog, Councillor Matthews. He appointed Michael as Chief of Police. Now, we know why."

The video is of the councillor having sex with a young girl, maybe around eighteen years of age. They pause from having sex to snort a line of white powder each and then get back to it.

"He has a wife and a nice little family. I'm guessing they don't know about this little addiction to pussy and coke," adds Maddocks. "The people of this town respect him because of his strong family values."

I call for Damien to come and see what we've found. He grins like we've won the lotto. "Let's arrange to meet the councillor. I'm sure it will make his day when we return this."

"Are you kidding? We could use this," I argue.

"We could, but if Michael holds nothing over the councillor, then surely, he can get rid of him as quickly as he appointed him. If there are less eyes on him, who the fuck will miss him when we go back for him and finish what we started?"

I laugh at Damien's cunning plan and pat him on the back. "Genius."

"Plus, I'm sure the councillor will be very grateful, which gives us brownie points too," he adds. "You need to speak to Ava, Gunner. It isn't what you think."

I shake my head. "I'm not ready, man. It took me this long to finally give us a go, and now, this."

"You're both too stubborn for your own good," he grumbles.

It's the early hours of the morning before I finally crawl into bed. My sheets smell of Cammie and it makes my stomach twist. Last week, things were so much clearer. What a difference a week makes. I desperately want to see Ava, but the thought of yet another man popping up has me keeping my stubborn arse in bed until I fall into a restless sleep.

I manage a few hours before the blaring sun shines through my window, waking me. I roll out of bed and decide on a run. That always helps clear my head. I run for an hour and then head back. It hasn't helped. I have a million questions to ask Ava, none of which are likely to make me feel any better.

Some of the guys are already up and about, the smell of bacon in the air. I grab a bottle of water and turn around, bumping straight into Ava. We stare at each other for a few seconds before she apologises and steps around me. One thing I hate more than arguing with Ava is being ignored by her.

"This gonna last?" I ask, and she turns back around, looking at me innocently.

"What?"

"You ignoring me, acting like nothing's happened."

"What do you want me to say? I didn't think it would last, it never does with you, so I guess I'm numb to it."

"Don't turn this on me. We're back to the same old fucking question, aren't we? Who's the daddy?"

Ava narrows her eyes. "Are you kidding?" she snaps.

"You heard Michael, he's not her dad."

"Wow, you really haven't clicked, have you?"

I take a deep breath to stop myself from losing my shit over her riddles. "It's you, Ashton. You're her dad." My mouth opens, but no words come out, so I close it again. "There was no one else, just you and Michael. I assumed it was him because he didn't use protection once and we did. If it isn't him, then it's you."

I feel around behind me for a stool and lower onto it, still staring at her in shock. "I assumed you knew that. I thought you were mad because you weren't happy about it," she continues.

I'm a dad. I'm Evie's dad. The words play on loop in my head, trying to make myself believe it. "I'm a dad," I eventually say, and she nods, a small smile playing on her lips. Hope fills my chest. They're mine . . . Ava and Evie are mine. "You're both mine," I say, and she gives a laugh.

"Slightly caveman of you, but yes, if you'll have us."

I stand and pull her towards me, wrapping my arms around her and burying my nose in her hair. I sigh and tell her, "I think you've just made me the happiest man in the world,"

EPILOGUE

Ava

"It's bad luck," yells Chloe, trying to push the bedroom door closed. Gunner shoves it, and she falls back, the door banging open. "Gunner!"

I turn to face him, and he inhales in surprise, taking in my attire. The white lace corset pushes up my B-cup breasts, giving me the perfect cleavage, and the garter belt holds up the stockings. I was just about to get into my wedding dress, and I'm glad I didn't, or I really would think it was bad luck.

He grabs me by the waist and pulls me against him. "Get rid of her, now," he whispers, nipping at my lower lip. I smile at Chloe, and she huffs, stomping out of the room and slamming the door.

"You've pissed off my maid of honour," I say, shaking my head and adding a smirk.

"I needed to see you, check you were definitely coming today," he says, running a hand around my corset, trying to find a way in. There is no way this baby is coming off—it took us twenty minutes to get me all tied in. I close my eyes when his fingers give up on the corset and run across the top of my white lace knickers instead. "I can't go all day and then all evening without being inside you. Especially now I've seen you like this."

He begins to rub small circles against my clit, and he smiles knowing that he has me exactly where he wants me. He moves my knickers to one side and runs a finger along my opening. I'm already drenched as he pulls his finger away, slipping it into his mouth.

"Just a quick one. I've got to get back to the bar before Damien sends out a search party." He grins, undoing his trousers.

"And who said romance was dead?" I grin, turning around and bending over.

Gunner lines himself up with my entrance and then pushes in, halting once he's fully inside me. "Last fuck as a bachelor," he says with a grin and then begins to move in and out at lightning speed. It's not long before we're both reaching our orgasm. He pulls me to stand and holds me against him, my back to his front. "I love you, Mrs. Gunn."

"I love you too, Mr. Gunn."

There's nothing perfect about me and Aston. It's been one fuck-up after another, and we've done too many things we regret. But out of the mess came our beautiful daughter, something we're both very grateful for.

We sat her down and told her the truth the minute she returned from her holiday. She'd never asked me about having a father. I think she'd always been so happy surrounded by the guys, it never occurred to her to ask. But when we told her the truth, she was so happy. She took to calling Gunner 'Daddy' right away, which relaxed him. He was convinced she'd reject him, but they've spent every day together since, learning all about one another. He's the most amazing father already.

As for Michael, Damien met with the councillor who appointed Michael as Chief. He was so happy to get the video that he now turns up regular to the clubhouse and is attending our wedding today with his wife and two daughters. He sacked Michael for his behaviour with Hayley. He did it all lawfully, of course, so Michael couldn't come back with anything. Something along the lines of dismissal due to indiscretions at work, which is against police force policy, especially for higher rank employees.

I haven't seen or heard from Michael since. I don't know if that's because he left town or whether Gunner and Damien took care of him. Either way I'm happy he's gone.

Walking down the aisle towards Gunner feels like an out-of-body experience. I'd dreamt of this moment for most of my life, never believing for one second it'd ever come true. And as he takes my hands in his and we exchange our vows, I finally see our future together working out. There'll be bumps in the road for sure, it's just the way we work, but we've sworn to stay faithful and work at our problems.

We finally get to the part we've been waiting for—exchanging a swoon-worthy kiss to the cheers of the club. We turn to the rows of guests, holding up our hands in unison. I think the brothers are just as relieved as we are to finally get to this point.

Now, we have a future to look forward to, one I've always dreamt of, with my one true love, Gunner, and our daughter, Evie. Our little family, together forever.

THE END

Read a sample of Cooper by Nicola Jane

COOPER

CHAPTER ONE

I straighten my pencil skirt. I chose the blue one because it wasn't as depressing as black, but now, I feel underdressed and not very formal.

"Well, Miss Coin, it was lovely to meet you. We'll be in touch."

The stuck-up woman in front of me stands, her black suit ironed to perfection. She must spend hours tending to that, I think to myself. She holds out her hand for me to shake, letting me know this meeting is over.

I know she won't be in touch. This is the eighth job I've interviewed for, and I haven't heard back from any of them. At this rate, I'm going to have to take Harper up on her offer of bar work.

I leave the office and pull out my mobile phone to call Harper, my best friend since forever. Our mums were on the same maternity ward, giving birth just one day apart. They began swapping birth stories, discovered they lived just two blocks away from each other, and soon became firm friends. The friendship continued even after Harper's parents moved away for a better life.

"Hey, sweetie, how did it go?" asks Harper. I can hear voices in the background, so she must be at work.

"Not good. The woman who interviewed me looked me up and down as soon as she saw me. I could tell she didn't like me."

"Mila, you're paranoid. I'm sure you did fine. Come to the bar and I'll make you some lunch."

I jump in my car and head to the bar where she works. My car is in serious need of some loving, so it's a miracle I make it. The beat-up red hatchback is my pride and joy, the one thing I saved up to buy during my time at college. It took a lot of waitressing to buy it and I feel a sense of pride that I did it on my own, which makes it harder for me to sell her now.

The car park is full of motorcycles when I arrive. A few bikers are leaning against the outside wall with cigarettes hanging from their mouths while they laugh and joke amongst each other. I used to feel intimidated by them, but since getting to know some of them, I realise they're not as bad as their reputation makes them out to be.

As I approach the doorway, Jase, a member of the Hammers Motorcycle Club, opens the door for me, standing back for me to pass. "Hey, Mila, nice to see you." He winks, looking me up and down with interest. "You're looking smart. You been anywhere nice?"

"A job interview, nowhere exciting."

He grins. "I can take you somewhere exciting."

I roll my eyes. He means no harm, but I'm pretty sure his wife, Kayla, will eat me alive if I touch her man. "Kayla is all the excitement you need, big guy," I say as I head on inside to find Harper.

There're bikers everywhere. Harper is leaning over the bar to talk to Kain, the club's Vice President. She's had a thing for him for months, but he doesn't seem interested, much to her disappointment. It's not like she's unattractive—that girl could cause a car accident with the amount of attention she gets. With her long blonde hair down to her rounded backside and bright blue eyes, she's like every man's wet dream.

I sit beside Kain, and Harper gives me a sympathetic smile. "Don't look so glum, sweetie. You'll find something soon, I'm sure," she says as she places a Diet Coke down in front of me.

"What you looking for Mila?" asks Kain, chugging back his beer.

"A job."

"Doing what exactly?"

"I just had an interview for a nanny position, but I don't think I got it."

"You good with kids?" he asks, a smile pulling at the corners of his mouth.

I shrug. "Yeah, I guess. I have lots of experience, but there just doesn't seem to be any jobs out there at the moment."

"You know, the Pres might need someone. Let me talk to him."

He's referring to Cooper, the President of the Hammers MC. Cooper is the scariest man I've ever met, though I've only actually met him twice. According to Harper, he keeps to himself most of the time, preferring to stay around the clubhouse rather than venture into the bar.

I watch Kain retreat as he heads into the clubhouse. His huge six-foot frame is nothing compared to his President, but he still fits snug in those Levi's, and I admire his backside as he walks away.

"Man, he is so fine. It doesn't matter what I do, the guy just doesn't show me any interest," huffs Harper, making no secret of the fact she's also watching his arse as he leaves.

"You need a cloth to wipe up the drool," I say with a smirk.

"You're not funny," she grumbles. "You see how hot he is, right?"

I nod. "He is gorgeous." He's tall and well-built, his muscles are as big as my thighs, and tattoos cover both arms. His hair is always tied back in a man-bun style, so I imagine it's at least shoulder-length. "Maybe you should pay him no attention. He must get sick of women swooning at his feet. Play it cool."

Harper ponders my suggestion while pouring a pint for Sam, one of the older members of the club. The door to the clubhouse opens and Kain pops his head through.

"Mila, come back here and see the Pres," he shouts.

I've never been in the clubhouse. Harper's been working here for six months now, and she said no one goes back there, not even her. It's strictly club members only unless you get invited.

We walk through a huge open-plan room with couches dotted about and two pool tables. It's not very inviting, but I'm sure it's ideal for the guys who hang around here. A blonde with straggly hair is sitting on one of the pool tables. Her bra is on show and she has short-shorts on, exposing her pale, skinny legs. She tracks my movements with narrowed eyes, a look of irritation on her face.

"Where the hell are you taking her, Kain? It better not be to Cooper's room." Her voice is raspy, like it will run out at any second.

"Shut the hell up, Carrie, and keep your nose outta my business."

A little boy comes running into the room making a siren noise at the top of his lungs. He skids to a halt in front of Kain, tipping his head back to look up at the large biker.

"Asher, stop making that goddamn noise. Your uncle will string me up," yells Carrie, jumping off the pool table and marching towards him. He looks at me with sad eyes, and I wonder if she's his mum. *Poor kid.*

We get to a red wooden door with the word 'President' painted in black. Kain knocks loudly and a gruff voice orders us to come in. Cooper sits behind a large oak desk with his boot-clad feet resting on top of it. His shoulders are straining under his tight, black T-shirt, and I wonder how something so big can fit into normal, human-sized clothes. He's engrossed in something on his mobile phone, so he doesn't immediately look up.

"Pres, this is Mila."

After a few more seconds, he raises his head. His piercing green eyes meet mine and he just stares. I fidget, I hate being stared at.

"No," he finally says, and then looks back at his phone.

"Come on, Coop. She's got loads of experience, and we need the help. The kid's running riot," says Kain, sighing.

"I said no. Now, get her the fuck out of here."

Cooper continues staring at his phone, and I feel a rage burn through my veins. How rude to not even ask me a question before dismissing me. I'm so sick of being turned away, I need a reason. *What am I doing that is so wrong?*

"Why?" I ask. My voice comes out quiet, almost a whisper, and I inwardly cringe. It sounded much louder when I said it in my head. They both look at me, and I suddenly feel that perhaps I shouldn't have spoken to him directly. Maybe in a motorcycle club there are rules about how to address the President, like rules for people meeting the Queen.

His face tells me he isn't used to being questioned when he's made his decision, and that felt like a very final decision.

"Because you aren't what I'm looking for," he grates out.

"But you didn't ask me anything. How would you know?"

He gives me an irritated look. "Get her out of here, Kain."

Kain goes to open the door but stops when he realises I haven't moved to follow him.

"I want a goddamn reason. I'm sick of being told no. I'm a good nanny, I have loads of experience, and kids love me. Is it the way I look? Am I dressed wrong?" He looks me up and down again, which grates on my last nerve. "Oh, just forget it. I'd rather sell my body than work here with someone as rude as you." I stomp towards the door. Kain raises his eyebrows with an amused look on his face and then leads me out of the office.

Carrie is still in the room. She has a hold of the boy's arm and he's crying. She's in his face, whispering angrily at him, when my protective side jumps to attention. "Let go of him right now." I march over to where they are, and the realisation hits me that I possibly just yelled at this kid's mother.

She looks at me in surprise but releases his arm. "Who the hell are you?" she demands, glaring from me to Kain.

I ignore her and pick the little boy up. Even if she is his mum, the boy is clearly distressed, and it breaks my heart. He must only be around three years old. He sniffles a few times, keeping his eyes fixed on me, then he wraps his arms around me and buries his dirty, tear-stained face into my neck. I smile, holding him tighter.

Carrie looks surprised. "He let you hold him," she mutters.

"Fuck," Kain gasps.

"Get back in here. Bring the kid with you," shouts a booming voice from behind me. I turn to see Cooper standing in his office doorway.

I go back in to his dark, depressing office, the manly vibe letting me know that Cooper is, without doubt, a man's man. He sits on the edge of his desk, his brow furrowed.

"That kid's been with me for a month now and not once as he let anyone touch him, let alone hold him," he says, his voice gruff.

I instinctively rub gentle circles on the boy's back. "Maybe if everyone stopped referring to him as 'the kid' . . ."

"Asher. His name is Asher," says Cooper in an almost apologetic tone.

The light snores tell me that Asher has fallen asleep, all that crying must have worn him out. I make my way over to the couch leaning against the office wall and gently lay him down. He stirs briefly before snuggling against the pillow. I pull a blanket from the back of the couch to cover him, taking a moment to stare at his dirty little face, wondering when he last got a bath.

"I need someone to live-in," says Cooper, bringing me back from my thoughts.

I turn to him. "I thought I wasn't right?"

"I reckon you'll last the week before you tell me to shove the job up my arse. The kid's a handful. He hardly sleeps, won't eat properly, and just races around, playing on his own."

I love a challenge, so I smile. "Where will I sleep?"

"You can have a room next to the kid. Anything you need, you go to Max. He's a prospect and his job is to run around. I'll pay you cash, weekly. You can have Sundays off. I'll get Max to show you around."

"Just Sundays?"

"Like I said, you won't last the week."

Cooper sticks his head out the door and shouts for Max, who appears in a flash, looking eager to please.

"This is . . ." Cooper pauses and looks at me.

"Mila," I say with a smile.

"She's Asher's new nanny. Show her to the room next to the kid's. Get her settled."

Max wiggles his eyebrows at me. "Not a problem, Pres." He grins, and I laugh, but Cooper doesn't look impressed.

"Off limits, especially to a prospect," he snaps.

We leave the office, turning left and heading through another door that takes us straight to a set of stairs. I follow Max up to the second floor. There're three doors along the landing, and he opens the first one.

"This is Asher's room."

I step inside. It's decorated in different shades of blue and there're posters on the wall of a cartoon character. A small bed, full of teddy bears, sits against one wall. There's an overflowing toybox in the corner of the room and a small bookshelf full of children's books. It isn't what I expected.

"Surprised?"

"A little."

"He cares about the kid. Just doesn't know how to look after him."

"Well, hiring somebody else to do it won't solve the problem."

Max leads me to the next door and flings it open. It's bright, with cream walls and a huge four poster bed. "Wow, this is really nice. Is this my room?" He nods as I step inside. The furniture is cottage style, also in cream, and there're intricate flowers hand painted onto the walls in random places. There's a double glass door that opens out to a small balcony. It overlooks a field which must be what the club backs onto.

"The Pres' room is the one at the end. He doesn't like to be disturbed, so you're best calling for me and I'll get whatever you need." He hands me a mobile phone. "This is your work phone. It has everyone's number that you'll need. If the Pres rings you, then answer. He hates to be ignored."

"I'll need to go home and get some things. Let Cooper know I'll be back tomorrow at nine and we can go through Asher's schedule."

"Schedule? He doesn't really have one. I can take you to get your things and bring you straight back."

"No, I need to speak to my parents and my boyfriend."

We head back downstairs. I get as far as Cooper's office door, and he appears. "Where are you going?"

"Home."

"Knew you wouldn't last the week," he mutters.

"I need to get my things. I'll be back tomorrow." He raises an eyebrow. "Well, Max will take you to get your things and then you can come straight back."

Max grins. "I already offered, Pres, but she wants to see her boyfriend."

A brief look of annoyance passes over Cooper's face. "I need you here tonight. I've made plans and need someone to watch the kid."

"I literally just took the job. I can't start straight away."

"Then forget it, I'll find someone else," he snaps, heading back into his office and slamming the door.

I'm pretty sure I'm his only option right now, but I need this job. I'm so over attending pointless interviews. "Fine," I huff. "Max, I have my car outside. I'll go and get my stuff and be back in a few hours. Let the grumpy bastard know."

Available from Amazon and Kindle Unlimited...

https://mybook.to/CooperSHS

A note from me to you

I'm a UK author, based in Nottinghamshire. I live with my husband of many years, our two teenage boys and our four little dogs. I write MC and Mafia romance with plenty of drama and chaos. I also love to read similar books. Before I became a full-time author, I was a teaching assistant working in a primary school.

If you'd like to follow my writing journey, head over to my facebook group, nj'sbookbabes.

Popular Books By Nicola Jane

The Kings Reapers MC

Riggs' Ruin https://mybook.to/RiggsRuin
Capturing Cree https://mybook.to/CapturingCree
Wrapped in Chains https://mybook.to/WrappedinChains
Saving Blu https://mybook.to/SavingBlu
Riggs' Saviour https://mybook.to/RiggsSaviour
Taming Blade https://mybook.to/TamingBlade
Misleading Lake https://mybook.to/MisleadingLake
Surviving Storm https://mybook.to/SurvivingStorm
Ravens Place https://mybook.to/RavensPlace
Playing Vinn https://mybook.to/PlayingVinn

The Perished Riders MC

Maverick https://mybook.to/Maverick-Perished
Scar https://mybook.to/Scar-Perished
Grim https://mybook.to/Grim-Perished
Ghost https://mybook.to/GhostBk4

Dice https://mybook.to/DiceBk5

The Hammers MC (Splintered Hearts Series)

Cooper https://mybook.to/CooperSHS
Kain https://mybook.to/Kain
Tanner https://mybook.to/TannerSH

Printed in Dunstable, United Kingdom